MONSTER, HUMAN, OTHER

ALSO BY LAUREL GALE

Dead Boy

MONSTER, HUMAN, OTHER

Laurel Gale

CROWN BOOKS
FOR YOUNG READERS
NEW YORK

Text copyright © 2017 by Laurel Gale
Jacket art copyright © 2017 by Emily Balsley

All rights reserved. Published in the United States by Crown Books for Young Readers, an imprint of Random House Children's Books, a division of Penguin Random House LLC, New York.

Crown and the colophon are registered trademarks of Penguin Random House LLC.

Visit us on the Web! randomhousekids.com

Educators and librarians, for a variety of teaching tools, visit us at RHTeachersLibrarians.com

Library of Congress Cataloging-in-Publication Data is available upon request.
ISBN 978-0-553-51012-6 (trade) — ISBN 978-0-553-51013-3 (lib. bdg.) — ISBN 978-0-553-51014-0 (ebook)

Printed in the United States of America
10 9 8 7 6 5 4 3 2 1
First Edition

For my husband, who once suggested
I write a book

Isaac Read had long ago mastered the art of unpacking. As he put his belongings away, he took care not to rip any of the cardboard boxes, which he would be using again soon enough. The entire process took less than an hour—a record for him.

The Reads' new one-story house resembled their old one. Generic furniture flattened the beige carpet underneath. Mildly pretty but uninteresting pictures, the type found in hotel rooms across the country, decorated the walls. In many ways, the rented house wasn't much different from a hotel. There was no point in buying a house to make their own, though;

not when the Reads would have to pack up and move again in another six months.

Mr. Read, tall and thin, with an angular face softened by his kind eyes and somewhat fluffy mess of light brown hair, knocked on Isaac's door before entering with a plate of peanut butter cookies. "How do you like your new room?"

"It's nice." Isaac took a cookie, still warm and soft.

"I think it's bigger than your last room."

Isaac's mouth was full, so he nodded his response. The room was a tiny bit bigger, but Isaac preferred small spaces.

"Did you see the walk-in closet?" Mr. Read pointed to the impossible-to-miss closet, already full of boxes, clothes, and other more secret items.

"Mmhmm." Isaac swallowed the last of his cookie and reached for another. "There was a spider in it."

Mr. Read's eyes widened. He edged away from the infestation in the closet. "Is it still there?"

"No. I killed it." Actually, Isaac had put it outside, but he knew his father would feel more comfortable thinking the tiny invader had died.

Indeed, Mr. Read's shoulders relaxed. "Have you heard from Darren?"

Isaac nodded. He wasn't allowed to use social

media—too many pictures—but Darren, one of his friends in Arizona, had sent him a text. Isaac could expect a few more, maybe even a couple of emails. Then the messages would stop. After all, he'd only known Darren for a few months—not nearly long enough for a lasting friendship to form.

"We could always move back there in the fall," Mr. Read said. "Then you could see him again."

"I guess. But . . ." Leaving his friends was hard enough. What if he returned and they didn't remember him? "I think I'd rather go somewhere new, like we always do."

"Okay. Have you thought about the classes you want to try?"

Isaac never attended public school. The biannual moving made homeschooling far more practical, though he did regularly sign up for other classes. He always took flute lessons, and he usually took some kind of art class. He liked sports, too. He was a little small for his age, but fast and agile.

"Maybe I could try sculpture." The thought of clay squeezing through his fingers appealed to him very much. "And soccer again."

Mr. Read frowned. "Soccer? Really? But remember Louisiana . . ."

Isaac remembered well enough. Right after scoring a goal, he'd noticed everyone staring at him, but at first he just assumed they were in awe of his amazing talent. It turned out his talent wasn't half as impressive as his tail, which had come out of his shorts and was sticking straight up.

They'd moved early that year.

"I'll tape my tail down. It'll be fine."

"If you're sure." Mr. Read held the plate out so Isaac could take another cookie. "Your mother's been summoned to a conference. She's running errands now, but she'll come back before catching her flight so you can say goodbye."

"A conference!" Isaac's tail, not currently taped into submission, shot up. "Can I go with her?"

"No, kiddo. You're too young."

Eleven years old hardly struck him as too young to start training, and it seemed far too old to be called "kiddo."

"But I'm going to be an ambassador someday. Shouldn't I learn? Unless you want me to fail." Isaac tried to keep a straight face as he said this, but he couldn't keep the corner of his mouth from twitching upward.

"Don't be silly. Of course I don't want you to fail.

4

And you won't. You'll have plenty of time to learn later—but not now. Not at your age. Relations between clepsits and humans are, well, tense, and this conference is no place for a little boy."

Isaac's tail fell. "Little boy." That was worse than "kiddo." He didn't see why his size should have anything to do with it. He was only a couple of inches shorter than most boys his age, which was probably average for a clepsit—although never having seen another one before, he couldn't be sure.

* * *

Later that day, Mrs. Read, a plump woman who liked to keep her dark red hair short and out of the way, transferred her clothes from a cardboard box to a suitcase.

"How long will you be gone?" Isaac asked.

"At least a week. Possibly longer."

Isaac glanced over his shoulder to make sure his father wasn't lurking nearby. "Dad said maybe I could go with you—start training for when I'm ambassador."

"He said no such thing, and lies like that will only land you in trouble when you're an ambassador, which isn't for many years now. You can start training when you turn sixteen, just as I did. Right now you need to be here, learning about human culture."

Isaac thought he could learn a lot more about humans if he didn't have to hide who he was from them, but he knew this wasn't a point worth debating. Clepsits knew all about humans, who had never bothered to keep a low profile, but preferred to keep their own existence secret—which meant that Isaac had to hide his real identity, too.

"How could you tell I was lying?" he asked. His mother always seemed to know.

"Your ears twitched. Can you hand me those socks?"

Isaac passed them to her. "I just want to meet others like me. Other clepsits. Will my dad be there?" He hesitated. "I'm sorry. I didn't mean—"

"It's okay." Mrs. Read tousled her son's white-and-brown-streaked hair. "Yes. Bronco of Snow, your birth father, will be there. I'm looking forward to talking to him—not just about the conference matters, but about you." She smiled. "And Wren."

"What is the conference about?" It wasn't a regularly scheduled one—those only happened on the winter and summer solstices of each year—which meant that some problem had arisen.

"There have been reports of voracans attacking people—both humans and clepsits."

"Voracans?" Isaac had never heard the word before. "What are they?"

Mrs. Read hesitated before answering. "Creatures, somewhat intelligent but very brutal, that live underground."

Isaac's tail shot up with excitement. "What do they look like? Are they another type of clepsit?"

"Oh, no, definitely not. I'll tell you more about them later, but honestly, they're very rare. I can't believe anyone thinks they're a real threat. The clepsits are probably just using this as an excuse to meet."

"Why?"

"They're angry about climate change, and pollution, and oil drilling, and overfishing. And they think I should be able to do something about it. I'll explain that I can't, but that the various human governments are trying. It'll be just like the last conference. Nothing new. Nothing to worry about."

Isaac nodded, but he *was* worried.

Clepsits had always felt threatened by humans. For good reason, too. Isaac had heard the cautionary tales, which his mother brought up whenever he got sloppy about taping down his tail in public. He knew that in the past, human mobs had attacked clepsits, accusing them of being witches or werewolves or something else equally ridiculous. That was why clepsits didn't want most humans knowing about them—and now Isaac wondered whether these new creatures, the voracans, stayed hidden underground for similar reasons.

But humans and clepsits still had to share the planet, so around 1800, when the Industrial Revolution resulted in fewer trees, more pollution, and a larger population, the ambassador program began. It was supposed to help humans and clepsits coexist. Sometimes Isaac wondered whether it was working.

"Will humans and clepsits ever get along?" he asked.

Mrs. Read checked her camera, which had a special case. She used nature photography as a cover for her travels and her real job as an ambassador, but the photographs always came out so stunning and sold so well that it might as well have been her real job. "I don't see why not. They have before. And we get along, right?"

"Yeah." Isaac smiled. "We do, Mom."

"I know it's hard for you. It was hard for me, too, growing up with the clepsits."

"Were they nice?"

"Oh, yes, very." Her eyes narrowed, and her smile vanished. "Well, some of them. Some were kinder than others, much like what you find among humans. Not everyone welcomed the presence of a human in their clan. But my parents—my adoptive parents—always took care of me. My mother used to sing me to sleep, and my father took me fishing, just the two of us, whenever I got fed up with the crowded burrow." Her smile returned. "You promise to be good while I'm gone, and to help your dad?"

"I promise. But I still wish I could go with you."

He was supposed to be learning about humans, but stuck inside the rented house, he couldn't do much. Keeping peace between the clepsits and humans would one day be his responsibility, and he thought it would be smart to begin preparing as soon as possible.

Wren of Snow poked her head into the ice-crusted hole and sniffed. She couldn't actually smell much of anything, but members of the Snow Clan always sniffed. She stood out enough without shunning the habits of her people.

As expected, the scent told her nothing. The entrance looked too small, but she always thought that of the hole that led to her clan's burrow. Still, this one was really tiny. It probably belonged to a burrow of marmots.

If her brothers had been around, they'd try to bring some of the marmots back for dinner. Wren could try, too, but she doubted she'd succeed on her own. The large rodents looked soft and funny, but marmots had teeth, and anything with teeth could bite. Wren had learned this from experience. Multiple experiences. She moved on.

The days were warming, and only sporadic clumps of winter's snow remained, but a chill still hung in the air. Wren tried to pretend it didn't bother her, but she couldn't stop her teeth from chattering or her skin from breaking out in goose bumps. She needed to find her burrow before night fell.

The next hole was larger. But was it hers? She poked her head inside.

A coyote emerged. It growled, and it might have attacked if not for the scent of clepsit on Wren. She backed away, and the coyote retreated into its cozy den.

An icy wind blew through the trees. Wren pulled her arms inside her dress. Made of fur, it should have been plenty warm, but it left too much of her hands and face exposed. Her mother kept offering to provide her with material for a new outfit—something with gloves and a scarf—but then her siblings and cousins would start teasing her. Wren would rather be cold than put up with that.

She found another hole about the size of the

entrance to the coyote's den, big enough to be her clan's. Her nose detected nothing, but her ears perked up at the sounds within. Howling. Screaming. Laughing. She hurried inside.

The entrance led to a tunnel. Deeper down, the aroma of meat mingled with the scent of vegetables. Wren's empty stomach grumbled, but she moved slowly. The tunnel would soon open into a nice burrow lit by oil lamps, but here the dark and narrow passage allowed little space. Although the others had no problem racing along the tight quarters on hands and feet, Wren crawled clumsily.

She reached the burrow, warm and cozy, and her body straightened into a more comfortable standing position.

The burrow housed a large family. Three families, actually, although they were all related. At the moment, many of the clepsits who lived there were away. They didn't worry about getting back before sunset. They were most likely visiting one of the neighboring burrows of the Snow Clan, places where Wren was always poked and prodded like a curiosity on display.

The clan had to house her. They had to feed her and clothe her and let her live among them. That was part of the treaty that had started the ambassador program. But no one had to accept her. No one had to want her there.

Some, like Aurora, made little attempt to hide this fact.

Aurora was one of Wren's aunts and the first mother of the Snow Clan, a privilege granted to her by her birth order. This had never struck Wren as a very logical way of deciding who had power, but it was a tradition that no one else questioned. Aurora and her husband, Iron, ruled the Snow Clan with absolute authority.

Wren had heard that humans voted to determine who was in charge, and although Aurora told these tales to show how backward and complicated human society was, Wren had always been fascinated by the idea of voting out her uncle and aunt.

There was no chance of that now, though, or of even avoiding her. Aurora, who rarely left the comfort of her burrow, stood in the cooking corner, where she was busy preparing a rabbit for the night's stew. She still bore her pale winter color, but brown had begun to streak her hair. "What is that stench? Has the meat gone bad?" She wrinkled her nose at Wren. "Oh. Never mind."

Breeze, who had been dicing dried vegetables,

growled at her sister. She was the second mother of the Snow Clan and Wren's own mother. At five feet four inches, she stood a good two inches taller than the average adult. Her hair had already turned almost fully brown, but her eyes were still blue and her skin was still pale. With her arms open, she turned to Wren. "Where have you been? I've been worried sick!"

Wren let her mother hug her. "I was just taking a walk. The others do it all the time."

"Yes, but they're . . ." She brushed a red curl from Wren's face. "You must be freezing. Let me warm you up a cup of broth."

"I'm not cold." She looked over her shoulder and saw that her three brothers, Coney, Colt, and Taurus, had stopped their game of bone dice to watch her. Kit, her sister, and Opal, her cousin, busied themselves by brushing each other's mostly white hair, but their occasional glances in her direction proved that they were listening. Garnet, Cobalt, and Mercury, more of her cousins, were wrestling as usual—the source of the howls and laughs audible from outside the burrow—but they were probably listening, too.

"I almost caught a marmot," Wren added, loudly enough for her eavesdropping audience to hear. "An entire colony of marmots."

"Almost? What happened?" Opal asked. "Maybe your hair scared them away. We could shave it off for you."

"No thanks."

Opal, always nimble on her feet, leapt up. Her long, thin fingers yanked at Wren's red hair. "Are you sure? You'd look better."

Kit, who mimicked everything Opal did, hurried over to pull Wren's hair, too. At least she didn't tug as hard. "Not good, but better," she said.

"Stop that," Breeze said, and Kit let go of Wren's hair at once. Opal did, too, though not as quickly.

"I like your hair," Coney said. He was small for his age, but with long arms and longer legs, a skinny boy who excelled at climbing trees. He held his tail in his hand, fidgeting with it. "It reminds me of a sunset, or fire."

"It *is* a little like fire. Maybe we should burn it," Kit suggested, causing Opal to laugh so hard she spit.

Aurora laughed, too, though more quietly than her daughter.

Breeze put down the knife she'd been using to chop vegetables, sticking the blade accidentally—or not—quite close to Aurora's fingers. "That's enough, everyone. Wren, why don't you check on the eggs?"

15

"No!" Opal gasped. Her tail rose straight up. "You can't let her near the unhatched."

"And whyever not?" Breeze demanded.

"She's—she's a human." Opal spat out the last word as if it was something evil. "They hurt our kind."

The boys stopped wrestling. Silence engulfed the burrow.

Breeze picked up the knife and resumed chopping vegetables. "Wren has never hurt any of you. And neither have any other humans, for that matter." She shot Aurora an angry look at this last point. "Humans and clepsits aren't that different, and as members of the host family, you're supposed to see that."

No one protested, but no one offered agreement, either.

Aware that the entire burrow was watching her, Wren approached the eggs.

The temperature was most important—the eggs couldn't get too cold or, less likely, too warm. After adding some wood to the fire, she made sure the burrow's small ventilation holes were clear so that the smoke could escape properly. She also checked the eggs for cracks or other signs of damage, and she made sure each one rested stably on the mat of soft leaves.

The already noisy burrow grew louder as the rest of

Wren's family returned. Four more cousins appeared: Willow, Olive, Elm, and Ash. Oak and Ether, the third father and mother of the clan, followed. Then came Bronco, Wren's father, the second father of the clan. Wren smiled at him, and he hugged her and lifted her above his shoulders so her head pressed against the roof of the burrow.

Much later, Iron returned. Wren's mother wouldn't have dared to stand up to Opal and Aurora if he'd been around. Luckily, he'd been spending more and more time away from the burrow recently, doing what, nobody knew.

Wren would never hurt the unhatched. If her cousin hadn't brought it up, the idea wouldn't even have occurred to her. Nevertheless, she couldn't deny that the eggs filled her with dread. The burrow was already crowded with enough clepsits who despised her. She was not looking forward to having more cousins around.

Isaac helped his mother carry her luggage to the living room.

He looked nothing like her or his father. He didn't resemble them in the summer, when his hair and eyes grew dark brown and his skin deep olive, and they had just as little in common in the winter, when his hair turned white, his eyes bright blue, and his complexion ghostly pale.

There were other differences, too, some far more significant than his variable tones. A tail. The lack of a belly button. Nails that grew fast and pointy and might better be described as claws.

Not only did Isaac not look like his parents, but he didn't look like anyone else he'd ever met, either.

He wasn't their son. He wasn't even human.

"What are the clepsits like?" he asked. "Really like?"

"The clepsits are a very noble race," his mother said. "You should be proud to be one of them."

Isaac already knew this. Mrs. Read had explained it on multiple occasions, ever since he was old enough to understand that having a tail wasn't normal among humans. She had also explained her role as an ambassador to the clepsits. Every generation, the human and clepsit ambassadors exchanged children—the result of a centuries-old treaty. These children would develop an in-depth understanding of the other species, and when they grew up, they would become the ambassadors of the next generation.

Which meant that Isaac's entire fate had already been decided for him.

"But what are they *really* like?" he persisted. "Are they like me?"

"Some more than others."

"What language do they speak?"

"English, in North America anyway. In some parts of the world, clepsits have their own language that they won't teach to humans, but here they just speak English." She checked the time on her smartphone. "I'm going to be late. We'll talk more when I get back, okay? I'm sure I'll have plenty of stories to tell you."

"Can't I just go with you?"

"No, not yet." She hugged him goodbye. "Behave while I'm gone. I love you."

"I love you, too."

She left. Isaac wanted to follow her, but he didn't. Halfway through his seasonal change, with brown-and-white-streaked hair, he looked too strange. He'd have to wait a little while, until he'd settled into his summer colors, before venturing outside.

It was hard not to feel like a prisoner sometimes. He tried not to complain, and he knew his life wasn't bad. It just didn't always seem like *his*. All the important decisions had already been made for him.

"Do you want me to bake some more cookies?" Mr. Read asked, maybe a little too cheerfully.

"Sure," Isaac said, with significantly less cheer.

He knew his father and mother loved him, and he loved them, too. Nevertheless, he couldn't help wondering what his biological parents were like, and how life would be among others like him. It would be nice, he imagined, not to have to hide what he was.

It would be nice to make his own choices. Nice, but impossible.

* * *

Isaac always decorated his bedroom in exactly the same way. Sports trophies lined the bookshelf. Green curtains covered the windows. Posters depicting woods and rivers hung on the walls. It helped to have at least a little consistency.

They moved every spring, then again every fall, and had ever since he was a baby. Now, at age eleven, Isaac was used to it, although that didn't make saying goodbye to his friends any easier.

His friends, of course, were the reason they moved, along with the grocery store clerks, the employees of the local miniature golf course, and his many instructors and coaches.

The tail and missing belly button he could hide under clothes, and his slightly shorter-than-average height wasn't the sort of thing that raised eyebrows. But the annual changes from pale to dark and then dark to pale would. Even if he dyed his hair—which he didn't want to do because the chemicals irritated him—his eyes and skin changed color, too, and there was no hiding that. If he stayed in one place year-round, everyone would realize how different he was. Everyone would ask questions he wasn't permitted to answer.

Relocating was the only way to keep his secret and his family safe. It was the only way to calm the clepsits' fears about what might happen if their existence became common knowledge among humans. Not being able to develop friendships that lasted longer than six months was just an unfortunate consequence. His parents had explained this to him before, and they didn't need to again.

And he did like his new bedroom, even if it was too large. The walk-in closet was like a smaller, cozier room. Curled up in a blanket, Isaac fell asleep there.

He had the usual dream. The forest beckoned him—its trees perfect for climbing, its dirt perfect for digging. He explored for many happy hours, but then the sun disappeared and the forest plunged into darkness. Suddenly he felt small and alone. His family had abandoned him long ago, but it had only started to bother him now.

All of this was normal—until a stench blew through the dream. It choked Isaac, and even in his sleeping state, he sensed that something was wrong.

"Is that the boy, the boy?" The voice had a grating quality, like nails scraping against metal.

"Perhaps, perhaps. We must watch him, we must."

Isaac awoke with a jolt. He sniffed the air. It smelled strange, like rotten eggs or sulfur. He got up, but even after searching the closet, and then the entire room, he could find no source of either the scent or the voices. By the time he gave up looking, the sulfuric smell had faded.

He scampered to the living room.

"Is everything okay?" his father asked, coming out of the kitchen. He had flour on his forehead.

"Yeah." Isaac decided to say nothing of the voices or the odor. There was no reason to bother his father with what he was beginning to realize must have been a silly dream. He forced a smile. "What kind of cookies are you making this time?"

Opal kicked in her sleep, and most of the time, she kicked Wren. Wren scooted as far away as she could, but the mat wasn't that large, especially when shared by five girls, and Opal's feet always found her. She considered moving off the mat, but the cold, hard ground would not make sleep come any easier. Not that she had the slightest hope of rest anyway, not while Kit's snores blared in her ears.

The clepsit girls awoke at dawn. Finally, with the mat all to herself, Wren fell asleep.

What seemed like just a few seconds later, Aurora

pulled the mat out from under her. "You'd spend the entire day sleeping if we let you. I suppose it's in your nature. Iron says humans build machines to do all their work for them. They even have contraptions that carry them around so they don't have to walk, never mind the pollution it produces. They're just too lazy to do anything themselves."

As first father, Iron had to travel through human territory occasionally, though not as often as Bronco. Bronco kept quiet about what he saw—Wren was supposed to be learning about clepsits, not humans—but Iron always came back with tales of the dirty humans and their disgusting cities, stories that Aurora managed to make worse with each retelling.

Wren wasn't convinced the human world sounded all bad, though. Sometimes she daydreamed of lazy days spent in well-heated rooms. She wouldn't mind having machines to wash her clothes and cook her food. If she lived with other humans, she wondered, would her life be easier? Would it be happier?

She rubbed her elbow, bruised from thudding against the icy ground, and scrambled up. "I didn't sleep well last night."

"You seemed to be sleeping fine a moment ago.

Snoring, too. I don't know how anyone gets any rest with you around." Aurora rolled up the mat and put it in the corner. The small room was rarely used during the day, so she was only doing it to make Wren get up.

In the main room of the burrow, a few bits of the fish served for breakfast remained. Wren stuffed them into her mouth.

Oak, third father of the Snow Clan, was showing the boys how to skin a rabbit. Aurora sat down next to Ether, who was teaching the girls how to sew pants. The last time Wren had worked on her stitching, Opal had lost her pincushion and decided that Wren's arm made a fine replacement.

Wren sat down with the boys. Smiling at her, Coney scooted over to make room.

Oak scowled. "This lesson isn't for girls."

Wren felt quite certain that he wouldn't turn away his own precious daughters, not that Willow or Olive would ever ask. They preferred to pretend that the rabbit in their stew was just another vegetable. "But Mother and Aunt Aurora skin rabbits sometimes," she said.

"That's different."

Of course it was different. They were clepsits, and she was a mere human. There was no point in arguing about it, though. Wren got up and joined the girls, none of whom scooted over for her.

"The leather is tough," Aurora was saying, "so you have to put a lot of force into it, but you still need to make neat, careful stitches. That's no problem for most clepsits, but Wren, well, just do the best you can with those clumsy hands of yours."

Wren took a pair of half-made pants and began sewing. She started with the tail hole, one of the trickier parts. Her muscles tensed, but the stitches came out almost perfect.

Opal snatched the pants from her. "Those are the ones I was working on! Here, you can have these." She handed Wren the pair she'd been sewing, which had a mangled mess of thread and torn leather where the tail hole should have been. Wren got to work undoing the stitches.

Aurora examined their progress. "Good, Kit. Good, Olive. You're getting better, Willow. Excellent, Opal. Oh, Wren, what a disaster. Look at how much leather you've wasted!" She took the pants. "Go find something else to do, will you? I can't deal with all the problems you cause."

Wren didn't argue. She had no desire to continue with the lesson. "Where's my father?"

"Bronco got called away to another conference," Aurora said. "Not that I see the point. You humans never do anything we ask."

Her father had left, and no one had thought to tell Wren? She never even got to say goodbye, and who knew how long he'd be away? "What about Mother?"

"She's outside collecting firewood. We've used up all our supply, due in no small part to her insistence on keeping the burrow warm for you. She's afraid you'll freeze, though I think a bit of chill might do you some good. It certainly couldn't do any harm. I always say, humans could use . . ."

Wren didn't stay to hear what humans could use. She scrambled up the narrow tunnel that led outside.

The rising sun shone down on what remained of winter's snow. As she looked for her mother, Wren stopped to pick up a stick here, a twig there. She hadn't thought to bring any twine to tie the wood together, so she wouldn't be able to collect much, but she could still help a little.

Something rustled in the bushes a few yards off, in a dark part of the forest where a thick canopy of trees kept the snow from melting.

"Mother, is that you?"

"We must find the human, the human. He said

she would be here." The voice was grating, nothing like her mother's sweet tones. It didn't sound like her father or Iron, either. Besides, her father was away, and Iron was hardly the type to make funny voices or hide in the bushes.

It was probably her cousins, disguising their voices as part of a prank.

"Mercury?" she demanded, in her strongest and most confident voice. "Cobalt?" She didn't know how her cousins could have sneaked past without her noticing, but she wasn't about to let them frighten her. "Garnet, I know that's you."

"Is she the human? Is she? She is cold, cold. He said she would be cold," said the grating voice, which actually didn't sound like her cousins, either. Maybe it was one of the Snow Clan members from a neighboring burrow.

It didn't matter who it was. Wren was in no mood to be teased by anyone.

"Yes, I'm the human. What of it?" She marched toward the rustling bush, which stank of rotten eggs. A copse of trees darkened the area, and she squinted in an attempt to see past the shadows. "What are you planning to do, throw those old eggs at me?"

A black shape burst from the bush.

A large ball of sticks, Wren thought, almost as big as she was and blackened by fire. The owner of the voice had thrown it at her.

But the ball of sticks moved with a purpose. It shifted forward like something possessed, Wren realized, not like something thrown. Each sharp needle twisted and turned until the mass took on the shape of a leg here, another there, and yet another there— arms and legs springing out, only to disappear after each step. Near the center of the mass was a squishy thing with two dark orbs that resembled eyes. Wren wasn't sure if she was looking at a face until it flashed an evil smile.

"The human, the human," it cried.

The mass of black spines sprang at Wren. She hurried backward, nearly tumbling, as the razor-sharp points tore at her dress and hands. One spike, longer and more flexible than the rest, extended from the thing's mouth and wrapped around Wren's neck.

A second mass of spines crept out of the bush. "You must not drink, no, no."

The spike uncoiled from Wren's head. "Just a sip, a sip."

"Not here, not here. We must take her with us. Later we shall have all we want, all, all."

"Mother!" Wren yelled. "Mother!"

Her cries received no response, and her struggling only forced the spines deeper into her skin. There was nothing for her, a weak human, to do.

No. She steeled herself. Human, yes, but not weak—no matter what her aunt said. Her fingers still clasped the wood she had collected. Though every movement met with sharp resistance, she forced her arm up and plunged the bundle of twigs deep within the black spiny beast.

Its body tried to twist, tried to turn, and tried to form more snatching limbs, but the needles couldn't move properly. The twigs had stopped the thing—but not for long. Any second, the thin wood would snap. It already creaked and bent.

Wren scrambled away. The second spiny beast chased after her, limbs emerging with each fast stride. It leaped forward, and Wren thought that she had lost for sure, but then it stopped.

"The light! It burns. It burns!"

Wren scurried farther from the bush. The sun beamed brightly where the trees didn't block it, forming a line between light and shadow: a line the prickly creatures didn't cross.

"It is no concern, no, no," said the one that had

attacked Wren. The twigs that had slowed it down now lay in splinters on the ground, but it didn't attempt another attack, not while Wren stood in bright daylight. "We have found her. We will return. We will." They retreated into the darkness of the bush.

Isaac struggled to play the pieces his various flute instructors had tried so hard to teach him. He plodded through the notes, and the tunes came out like a chore, boring and despised.

Once he had slogged through the three songs he was supposed to master, he forgot about the sheet music and began to improvise. Now the music flowed naturally. The tune became wild, chaotic even, then slow and sad. His eyes closed and images of vast forests filled his mind. Although he had no audience at the moment, others had told him before that they too pictured wild and unending woods as he played.

"Is it him? Is it? Is it?" The music nearly drowned out the voice, but Isaac's ears caught the soft, grating sound. "We must be certain, certain."

Isaac had been playing longer than he'd realized, long enough for the sun to sink below the horizon. His room had grown dim. He usually had no fear of the dark, but he found himself rushing to the switch to turn on the light.

This was the second time he'd heard the voices, but the first time he'd heard them while fully awake. The first time he couldn't pass them off as a bad dream.

"Too bright, too bright."

The smell of rotten eggs filled the room. Isaac sniffed the sulfuric air, but he couldn't pinpoint the source. He scanned the room and saw nothing. "Who's there?"

"We would ask the same. Are you the clepsit? Are you?"

"No." The lie came without thought. Isaac couldn't reveal what he was to anyone, so he certainly wasn't about to confess to a strange, smelly voice.

The stench faded. Isaac fled his room.

"Is everything all right?" his father asked, smiling as Isaac bounded through the hall.

"No. I—" Isaac stopped himself. In the bright

34

living room, his heartbeat slowed to its normal rate. Although he now knew for certain that the voices had been real—not a mere nightmare—they nevertheless seemed very distant.

Isaac weighed his options. If he told his father the truth, one of two things might happen. His father might not believe the story, which would make Isaac angry. On the other hand, his father might accept that something was stalking the house, which would make him worried. Terrified. Neither outcome would help Isaac much.

For as brave as Mr. Read tried to be, and as hard as he tried to learn about the world his son came from, he knew little outside the realm of humans. And if spiders in the closet frightened him, how would he handle actual monsters lurking in the shadows?

And Isaac *did* suspect some sort of monster. What else could produce such a horrible stench? Or hide in the darkness before disappearing completely? Or know that humans shared the planet with other beings?

He wondered if they could be the voracans his mother had mentioned—the creatures that lived underground and had been attacking people recently. He could ask his mother when she returned from the conference. Until then, he could handle the situation himself. The monsters were looking for a clepsit, so he would make sure not to identify himself as such. It hardly ever came up in conversation with his father, anyway.

"I'm just thirsty." Isaac went to the kitchen to pour himself a glass of juice.

***

In no hurry to return to his room, Isaac stayed in the living room while his father made pasta. After dinner they played a video game, a virtual car race that Isaac had long ago mastered—there was plenty of time to practice when his seasonal color changes kept him inside. He let his father win, though, because it always made him happy.

It also made the game last longer—longer, but not forever. Eventually, Mr. Read put down his controller. "I'm going to do the dishes, and it's time for you to get ready for bed."

Remembering that the voices had complained about the brightness, Isaac grabbed a flashlight. Then he took a deep breath and steeled himself. He'd have to return to his room sooner or later. Putting it off would just make his father ask questions. Besides, there was something he needed.

Isaac kept the book hidden. No one had ever forbidden it—not directly. But he suspected that if his parents learned about it, they would not approve. After all, he was supposed to be learning about humans, not clepsits, and the clepsits were a secret kept from most of humanity. If this book got out, so would the secret.

Except, Isaac reasoned, no one would believe the book. People would assume it to be a mere fantasy. There was no real danger. He was doing nothing wrong.

Despite this sound logic, he never looked at the book when his parents were around. Instead, it stayed buried at the bottom of a box of puzzles and games, which he kept in his closet. He had titled it *An Inventory of Bugs Seen in My Room* so that his parents wouldn't be tempted to peek inside if they ever happened upon it.

It was actually a journal in which Isaac wrote everything he learned about clepsits, as well as several plants and beasts unknown to humankind.

Someday, when Isaac was ambassador, he'd get to meet members of each clepsit group, and he'd get to see the various species of exotic flora and fauna first-hand. But for now, he had to content himself with speculative drawings and incomplete descriptions.

Every time his mother mentioned a group of clepsits, he later recorded the information in his book. He wasn't much of an artist, but he drew, erased, and re-drew until he got it right, and wrote captions to clarify anything not made obvious by the sketch.

Without even looking at it, he knew that the first page detailed the northern clepsits, highlighting their short, wiry builds, long tails, and sharp nails. There were two pictures: one for the pale winter phase, and one for the dark summer phase. This was the group Isaac belonged to, and its entry was the most detailed.

The second page, he remembered, featured the Antarctic clepsits, with their large frames covered by thick coats of fur. The tropical arboreal clepsits, green with prehensile tails perfect for swinging from trees, took up the next page, followed by the aquatic group, who were blue with webbed hands and feet.

The animals and plants included rare antlered rabbits, flying serpents, and glow-in-the-dark underwater weeds that made excellent paint. There were others, too, but Isaac hadn't gathered enough information for much of a description. He had a few notes and a couple of partial sketches, but nothing much. The most recent entry was for the voracans, and it contained only what his mother had told him before leaving for the conference.

As far as he could remember, his mother had never mentioned creatures that smelled like rotten eggs or shunned the light. It was unlikely he'd forgotten anything—he practically had the book memorized— but he thought he'd leaf through the pages again just in case.

Armed with a flashlight, he opened the door of his walk-in closet and stepped inside.

A foul stench assaulted his nostrils. Something black and sharp lunged at him. It was just a ball—a terrible orb of black needles weaving in and out with no limbs to grab him. But just as he told himself this, arms appeared and grabbed his foot. He fell back from the door and kicked, and the thing ended up with only his shoe. He shined the flashlight at the creature, which retreated into the darkness of the closet.

Isaac approached the closet again.

Black needles pulled up a corner of carpet, revealing a hole in the floor, into which the creature disappeared. Isaac grabbed his shoe and threw it at the thing, but too late. The monster had gotten away.

Isaac moved a plastic bin, heavy with the toys and books inside, over the hole.

Pieces of paper littered the floor. Examining the scraps, Isaac recognized an image here, a word there. The torn paper came from his book. The creatures, whatever they were, had been looking for a clepsit. That was what they'd said earlier in the day. Isaac had denied being one, but now they had seen his secret book—a book that only a clepsit, or someone very close to a clepsit, could have the knowledge to write.

The thing had left, but it would return. Its entrance had been blocked, but it could find another.

The light streaming from Isaac's flashlight suddenly seemed very weak.

Upon hearing Wren's screaming, Breeze dropped the wood she'd collected. The two of them found each other at the burrow's entrance.

"Are you okay?" Breeze asked.

Wren nodded unconvincingly.

Inside the safety of the burrow, everyone listened in silence as Wren told them about the attack. After she had finished, they remained silent.

"Well," she said. "What do you think it was?"

"A whopper," Aurora said.

Wren opened her mouth to ask what type of creature a whopper was, but she stopped herself just in time. Her aunt meant "whopper," as in a tall tale. A flight of fancy. An untruth. "I'm not lying! I saw it! Two of them! They attacked me! See?" She stretched out her arms so they could see where the creatures had scratched her with their long, needlelike appendages.

"You probably ran into a tree," said Iron, who had returned to the burrow shortly after Wren. "Or else you did it to yourself on purpose to gain attention. I was in the forest, too, and I didn't see anything amiss."

Wren's face turned as red as her hair, and her hands balled up into fists. Her mother stroked her head, a gesture meant to calm her. The first father could say whatever he wanted, and anyone who tried to challenge him risked expulsion from the clan.

But Wren had the truth on her side. "I did not do it to myself! Something attacked me! I fought it off, and I'll fight anyone who calls me a liar, too."

Her mother stopped stroking her head and started holding her back.

"I'm certain you will." Iron smiled. "So like a human to turn to violence at the first sign of disagreement."

"Clepsits are violent, too," Wren pointed out. They were always killing rabbits or wrestling each other.

"We hunt for food, and we work together to

sharpen our hunting skills. Humans fight each other for power, for sport." He sighed. "Perhaps if clepsits had more of that warring instinct, *we* would dominate the planet and *humans* would live in hiding. We should be more like the humans."

Aurora gagged. "That's a horrible thing to say!"

"It sounds like a voracan," Oak said.

Wren had heard of voracans before, mostly through stories that her siblings and cousins whispered late at night. Foul creatures that stank of sulfur—of rotten eggs—the voracans lived underground, far below the clepsit burrows. That didn't mean clepsits were safe, though; when food became scarce in the crowded depths, the voracans went up in search of prey.

Wren had always pictured the voracans as ratlike creatures, or possibly as giant worms with rows upon rows of sharp teeth, but never as the twisting balls of spines that had attacked her. More importantly, she'd never actually believed the tales. They'd merely been stories meant to frighten her. At the very least, they'd been exaggerated. Hadn't they?

"Don't be silly," Aurora said, her voice a little too fast, a little too high-pitched. "What would voracans want with Wren? She's making up the story to get attention, just like Iron said."

But Oak wasn't convinced. "Isn't the conference Bronco's attending about voracans? They've been attacking people recently."

"Those are just silly rumors," Iron said. "Wren must have heard them and decided to use them in her story."

Wren hadn't heard the rumors, and she wasn't making things up, but for once she kept her mouth shut. She was too busy thinking to argue. The scary stories were true after all. Voracans were real, and for some reason, they had taken an interest in her.

But no one believed her. Which meant no one would protect her.

It didn't matter. She could protect herself.

"We've wasted enough time on this nonsense, and we still don't have any wood," Iron said. "Breeze, you need to prepare lunch. Wren, you can go collect the firewood."

Wren gulped. Was he really going to send her back out there? When she'd thought about having to protect herself, she hadn't imagined she'd need to start so soon.

Coney took her hand. "It's okay. I'll go with you."

"You don't believe her story, do you?" Iron snarled.

"I want to help her with the firewood," Coney said, evading the question. "We need a lot, and you know she can't carry much."

Iron eyed him with suspicion. "Fine."

After grabbing some twine to bundle the firewood, Wren and Coney left the cozy burrow. The dark, narrow tunnel that led outside seemed even darker and narrower than usual. Coney went first, even though Wren offered (quietly, and only once) to take the lead.

Outside, the sun beamed bright and high in the blue sky. For the first time in many months, no cold breeze chilled the air. Small patches of snow still stubbornly clung to the bases of trees, but these were melting quickly. An unseen bird sang a sweet song.

"I wasn't lying," Wren said. "I was attacked. By voracans."

Coney nodded. "I believe you."

"Then why didn't you say so to Iron?" Wren demanded, although she already knew the answer. Coney had always been kind to her, but he'd never stood up to the others. He had never risked getting in trouble.

"Iron wouldn't have let me come with you if he knew I believed you. I wanted to help you."

Wren supposed that was true, even if it wasn't the full truth. "The voracans that attacked me don't like direct sunlight."

Coney picked up a small branch. "That's because they usually spend their entire life underground, where it's dark."

The ample sunlight made Wren feel warm and safe, and they had no trouble staying out of the shadows.

After scouring the forest for hours, they found the bundle Breeze had dropped and collected another bundle on their own. It wasn't much, though—enough for a week, maybe two if they stretched it out. As spring took over, they'd need less wood for warmth, but they'd still need fire to cook. They'd have to cut down a tree—something clepsits always tried to avoid.

A lot of wood had been used to keep the eggs warm, but Aurora would blame Wren and her low threshold for the cold.

A roar of flowing water broke the quiet stillness of the forest. They had reached the stream, which meant they had wandered farther than Wren had realized.

"I guess we should go back," Coney said.

"Yeah." It might have been her imagination, but she thought she had caught a whiff of sulfur. They started walking toward the burrow.

"Wait." Coney stopped. "Listen."

Wren had heard nothing over her heavy footsteps. Once she paused, though, even her pitiful human ears could detect the sound. The voices were farther away than they'd been before, but just as grating. Just as horrible.

"We'll never get her if she stays in the light," one of the voices said. "If she's never alone. Never, never."

"Do not worry," came the screeching reply. "The others have found the clepsit boy, and we only need one. The clepsit boy. The clepsit boy."

Coney and Wren ran the rest of the way home.

Only a couple of white hairs were left. Isaac told himself that it didn't matter. One seasonal change had ended, but another would begin in a mere six months. There was no reason to get excited. He certainly didn't want to rush out to make friends that he'd have to leave again so soon.

But as hard as Isaac tried not to care, it did matter to him. He plucked the few remaining white hairs, leaving a perfectly ordinary head of dark brown locks. With his tail taped down under his jeans, he looked more or less normal.

"I'm going to the park down the street!"

"Okay," his father said, "but come home before it gets dark."

"I will." He hadn't heard—or smelled—the monsters in several days, but that didn't mean they weren't still lurking about, waiting for the lights to go out so they could catch him.

"Good. There'll be a surprise waiting for you."

Isaac stopped. "What is it?"

"A surprise—which means I can't tell you about it now. Go along. Have fun, and call me if you need anything."

"Okay."

Isaac debated what to bring. He didn't know what the other kids would be doing, and he wanted to fit in. In the end, he decided to take his bike, a soccer ball, and a backpack full of chocolate bars. In other words, his standard introduction kit.

He wouldn't be making real friends, he reminded himself. They'd be temporary friends—no one to get attached to. After all, he'd have to leave again in a few months. He was there to learn about humans, but because he wasn't one himself, there would always be a barrier between him and the kids he met. It was best to keep that in mind, or else the next move would be that much harder.

He couldn't form close friendships or tell anyone who he was, but that didn't mean he couldn't have a little fun. At the very least, it would be nice to get out of the house.

The warm Saturday afternoon had brought people to the park in droves. There were plenty of kids, but he couldn't just go up to them and start talking. He rode around on his bike for a while before stopping a few yards away from a group of three kids around his age.

Sitting on the grass, he removed his soccer ball from his backpack, which had a mesh pouch specially designed to hold it. After kicking the ball a few times, he let it roll over toward the three kids.

One of them, a somewhat chubby boy with very short hair, picked it up. He was going to kick it back so Isaac didn't need to go over, but he did anyway. That was, after all, the entire point.

"Thanks." Isaac caught the ball under his foot. "You play?"

"Not really."

The other boy, who was small with dark skin and glasses, grinned. "He means, not unless it's a video-game version of soccer. Probably one he programmed, too."

The girl laughed so hard she snorted. She had long brown hair, worn in a ponytail. Her braces glinted in the sunlight. "Can you imagine Justin playing actual sports?"

The chubby kid—Isaac took it he was Justin—was laughing, too, so Isaac allowed himself a couple of chuckles. "Do you want some chocolate?"

They did. Of course they did. Isaac had discovered long ago that chocolate was among the fastest ways to make friends (temporary friends) with humans. While Isaac handed out the chocolate bars, the girl introduced herself as Sara, the chubby boy as Justin, and the bespectacled boy as Ryan.

"I'm Isaac," he responded. "If you don't like sports, what do you do for fun?"

They showed him the cards they'd been playing with, which were nothing like normal cards. They represented different actions or monsters—most of which Isaac knew for a fact didn't really exist (he'd asked his mother).

"Which school do you go to?" Justin asked.

Before Isaac could answer, Sara asked, "How old are you?"

"I'm eleven. I don't go to any of the schools here. My family just moved into town, and I'm home-schooled."

They told him that they were eleven, too, except for Justin, who had just turned twelve. They went to one of the local middle schools, and according to Ryan, Isaac had caught a lucky break by not attending. "The food's awful, and even the teachers are bullies."

"It's not that bad," Sara said. "You're just mad because you couldn't get out of P.E."

"Heck yeah I am. And gluten intolerance is a serious issue. Everything in the cafeteria is filled with gluten! I bet there's even gluten in the air."

Isaac wasn't sure what gluten was, but he nodded in sympathy anyway.

They invited Isaac to play cards with them. Because he didn't have his own deck, he had to team up with Ryan, which was probably good since Isaac didn't understand the rules.

"Maybe you can help him," Justin said. "Believe me, he needs all the help he can get."

"That's not—" Ryan started. "Well, yeah, okay, that's true. But unlike you, I don't devote every waking second of my life to this game."

"Yeah," Sara agreed. "Because you have more important things to do. Like drooling over your sister's friends."

Ryan nodded. "Exactly."

They played until the sun started to dip below the horizon. Sara won, but stuffed with chocolate, everyone seemed happy.

"I have to go," Isaac said, wishing he'd brought a flashlight with him.

Justin looked at the setting sun. "Yeah. We should be going, too. But maybe we'll see you again next week. We come here every Saturday if the weather's all right. It's the only place we can play without being harassed about homework and chores and stuff."

"Cool," Isaac said. "And, you know, if the weather's bad—if you want—we could hang out at my place, too. My parents are cool."

They said that sounded great, so he gave them his address, and they exchanged phone numbers.

"You have your own phone?" Sara grabbed Isaac's smartphone.

"Yeah. My family moves around a lot, so a landline doesn't make sense."

She entered her number and proceeded to check out the apps. "My parents say I can't have one until I'm sixteen. Something about data charges—a lame excuse since most plans are unlimited. Justin keeps forgetting to finish the phone he promised to build months ago."

"You keep forgetting to give me the money for parts," Justin said.

"If I had that kind of money, I would buy a phone. And you have plenty of spare parts lying around your room." Sara handed the phone back to Isaac. "We'll see you next week."

"Okay," Isaac said, smiling, though not too brightly. He'd made friends, but—he reminded himself—not real friends. They were temporary friends. Acquaintances, in fact—just people to hang out with until the next move. No one to get attached to. No one to get excited about.

Frequent moves weren't the only reason he couldn't get close to anyone. People accepted him when they thought he was one of them, albeit with oddly long arms and slightly off features. But if they knew the truth—that he wasn't even human—they'd reject him in a second. He was sure of it.

He'd never know for certain, though, because even if he wanted to tell someone, the clepsits would never allow it.

In the past, the occasional village that had happened upon clepsits had reacted violently, with pitchforks and torches. Civilization had come a long way since then, but that didn't mean humans wouldn't respond with the same fear and hate that had driven them before. Modern technology—like videos to spread the news all over the Internet—meant things could get a lot worse.

But temporary friends beat no friends. Isaac's smile grew a little bigger.

* * *

As Isaac walked home, his phone rang. "Hi, Dad. I'm almost there."

"Good." He sounded relieved. "Do hurry."

"Why? Is something wrong?" It wasn't even dark yet, not fully.

"No. Just hurry."

Isaac broke into a run. His father was lying. Something was wrong. Why else would he call so early?

Then Isaac saw why. The pale green electric sedan was parked in the driveway. His mother had returned.

Isaac's already fast pace increased. By the time he

burst through the front door, he was out of breath, but this didn't stop him from tackling his mother with a great big hug. "How was the conference?"

"My plane was overbooked, and then I got held at customs—a silly misunderstanding over a clepsit supplement I'd forgotten I had on me. I would have been back two days ago otherwise. Then the woman sitting next to me coughed on me all the way here. I know the clepsit rails have problems of their own, but I think I actually prefer the days when human ambassadors were allowed to use them."

"What about the conference?" Isaac asked, pretty sure that all this talk about the plane was meant to distract him from the real event.

"It was good. Tense, but good. I had a lot of time to talk to Bronco. He's very interested in your flute playing—says he plays, too—though the piv—the clepsit flute—is a little different." Mrs. Read handed Isaac a small wooden figurine. It depicted two clepsits with their tails looped together in the clepsit symbol of good luck. "He carved it for you himself."

Isaac found a special spot for it in his room, right next to his soccer trophy. Then Mr. Read served dinner—a chicken and cheese casserole—and everyone had seconds. After dinner they played board games, and without anyone noticing, bedtime came and went.

By the time Isaac finally crawled under his covers, exhaustion consumed him. The events of the day replayed in his mind as he drifted off to sleep, and he was only vaguely aware of his mother turning off the light. A thought nagged at him—*the light has to stay on*—but he was too tired and too happy to remember why.

* * *

Hundreds of spines stabbed Isaac's flesh. He jolted awake. Something was pinning his mouth closed, and his scream came out muffled. The thick stench of sulfur choked him. The spines dragged him from his bed and across the floor.

His eyes adjusted to the darkness quickly. He saw the creature that had him: a monster that consisted of nothing but quills of various sizes. Another spiky beast shuffled in front of him, a third behind him. When they reached the door, the first one thrust out a cluster of quills to form a hand, and the hand turned the knob.

After checking on the stew, Wren got to work grinding the acorns, which would later be made into a nutritious paste that hatchlings loved.

"I can help," Coney offered.

Iron grabbed him by the tail. "You most certainly cannot. Cooking is women's work. Now practice wrestling with your brothers and cousins. I won't have a nephew who doesn't know how to fight."

Coney did as he was told, as always.

Wren didn't mind the work, pressing a round stone against a flat one and pulverizing the acorns caught between. The rhythmic motion relaxed her, something welcome in a burrow now filled with the cries of four hatchlings. She'd choose cooking over babysitting any day, not that Aurora would ever give her the option. Dirty human hands weren't allowed anywhere near her precious offspring. Her hands were apparently good enough to prepare the food, though.

Besides, if Coney really wanted to help, he'd try to convince the others that the voracans were real. Technically, he hadn't caught a glimpse of the prickly monster, but he believed it had been there. Maybe if he told the others he'd seen it—only a tiny fib—they'd believe, too. As it was, they just assumed that he was gullible and she was an attention seeker.

With a few more angry poundings, the last of the acorns became a fine meal. She put it aside. While the stew simmered, she didn't have much else to do, but she busied herself by stirring the pot. That way everyone would leave her alone.

The hatchlings crawled toward the kitchen corner. The three girls and one boy still had the soft fur of a clepsit newborn—a protective coat that would disappear by the second or third month of life, when they would receive their names. They stumbled on their untested legs, their tails wagging behind them. One of the girls found a piece of dried mushroom that had fallen onto the floor. She picked it up with her tiny hands and examined it.

Maybe these hatchlings wouldn't grow up to be as mean as their older sister. Surely Opal had never been this cute.

Wren reached down to retrieve the fungus.

"What are you doing, Wren?" Aurora grabbed the mushroom. "Are you feeding this to her? She's too young to eat this. She could choke on it."

"I know. I was just—"

"You know?" Aurora interrupted. "And you're giving it to her anyway? Are you trying to kill her?"

"No. No! It was on the floor—"

"You're feeding her scraps from the floor? You want her to get sick, too?" Aurora picked up her daughter. "Stay away from my children. Or else."

The stew didn't need any more stirring. Wren stomped off to the girls' sleeping room, the one room where she could expect a little privacy at this time of day.

But the room was already occupied. Bronco, who had been sleeping on the mat, opened his eyes and lifted his head.

"Oh, sorry, Father, I—What are you doing in here?"

He smiled, and the smile turned into a yawn. "It's the one place I thought I wouldn't get caught. Iron wants me to tell him everything that happened at the conference, but I just got back this morning. You'd think he'd let me relax a little before he started badgering me for details." He yawned again. "The conference really wore me out."

"Was it that bad?"

"No. Just a little tense. Traveling through the tunnels is always tiresome, too. I think I prefer human airplanes. They get snacks and a movie. It's faster, too." He patted the mat, signaling that she should sit beside him. "But what about you? Why'd you come here? Trying to hide out like me?"

"Yeah. I'm hiding from Aunt Aurora. Now she's accusing me of attempted murder."

His tail shot up. "Attempted murder? What happened?"

"Nothing. It's just Aurora being Aurora." Wren leaned backward until her head hit the mat. "It's not fair that she gets to be first mother and Iron gets to be first father. You and Mother are far smarter. And nicer. And better smelling."

"Your aunt and uncle don't smell bad. And you know that intelligence and kindness have nothing to do with it. Aurora is the first-hatched daughter of the first-hatched daughter of the clan, so her family is first, and will remain so unless she decides to give up the position."

"That's never going to happen." Wren knew that Aurora liked bossing everyone around too much to consider it. Not that Wren would ever give up the position, either, if it were hers. But a human could never be first-hatched.

"Now what's this I hear about a voracan?" Bronco asked. "Were you really attacked by one?"

Wren sat upright. "Of course I was! You can't accuse me of lying, too!"

"I'm not. I believe you, I promise. Now keep it down or we'll both lose our hiding spot." He hesitated. "At the conference, many clepsits spoke of voracans coming up to the surface to feed more often. Even some humans have noticed it. But you said they wanted you in particular, right? I don't understand why they would be so interested in you."

"Well, they were." And for all Wren knew, they remained so. She had been staying out of the dark as much as possible, especially when alone, which wasn't often. She stood. "I need to check on the stew."

Hopefully she'd manage to do so without being accused of murder again.

The tunnels offered no source of light. In the utter darkness, even Isaac, with his keen clepsit vision, could see nothing. He sensed their general direction, though: down, always down.

His captors spoke sometimes—always to each other, never to Isaac.

"Hungry," one said. "So hungry, so hungry."

"Yes, yes," another one said. "Just a sip, a sip."

"No," said the third one, the one holding Isaac. It used its quills to jab the others. "We must keep him alive. Remember the plan, the plan."

"We remember, but we're so hungry, so hungry."

Hunger gnawed at Isaac's stomach, too. How long had he been down there? Five hours? Two hours? Thirty minutes? It was hard to tell time stuck inside a pitch-black nightmare.

Regardless, his parents would soon be wondering where he was. When they couldn't find him, they might assume he'd run away. Had he seemed unhappy recently? The move always depressed him, as did waiting for his seasonal change to finish so he could venture outside their generic new house, but he tried not to let it show.

Things had been getting better, too. The last day had been perfect. His parents must have noticed how happy he'd been.

They would see the blood on his sheets, spilled when the creatures grabbed him with their hands of needles. They'd see the signs of struggle, and they'd know he'd been taken. Then they'd start searching for him. They might be looking already.

But would they know where to look? How could they find him when he himself had no clue where he was? Even if he managed to escape his captors, he doubted he could find his way out.

He had to start paying better attention. His vision wouldn't help him much, but he still had his sense of smell, as well as pretty good senses of balance and direction, if he could only push aside his fear and discomfort enough to focus.

"Where are we going?" he asked.

"Home, home."

Not Isaac's home, obviously. "Where do you live?"

"Deep underground, but not for long, not for long." The creature's grip loosened. "Soon, the surface will be ours, ours."

Isaac could now move more freely, though not freely enough to escape. "Why do you want it?"

"We need more room, more, more. More food, more, more. There are so many of us."

"So many, so many," the other two creatures echoed.

A chill coursed through Isaac. These things had an underground lair, and they had overcrowded it. Once Isaac got there, surrounded by hundreds or even thousands—perhaps millions—of the spiky monsters, all hope of escape would vanish. He jerked back the way they had come, but he barely moved an inch before the spines dug deeper into his skin.

"What are you?" he asked, although he suspected he already knew.

All three spoke at the same time, each giving a different answer.

"The nightmare that waits for you in the dark, the dark."

"The hunger that crawls through the earth, the earth."

"The planet's future masters, future masters."

Isaac gasped as the creature's spines cut his shoulder. "But *what* are you? You're not human. You're not clepsit. Are you voracan?"

"Yes. Yes. We are the voracans. Yes. Yes."

"We must hurry, hurry. The next phase of plan shall begin soon, soon."

As their pace quickened, their grip on Isaac tightened. He couldn't wiggle free, and his attempts exhausted him. How much blood had he lost? Although none of the cuts on his body were deep, they were numerous.

He did his best to track his forced journey, but in the utter darkness, only one thing seemed certain. They were still going down.

After another restless night of listening to her sister's snores and avoiding her cousins' kicks, Wren spent the morning sleeping. No one bothered to wake her, so it was quite a long time before she pried herself from the mat.

Imagining another one of her aunt's lectures on human laziness, she considered lying there for a while. Maybe it wouldn't be so bad, though. Aurora might be too busy with the hatchlings to notice the late rising.

Wren, still groggy with sleep, staggered into the main room.

She found the room strangely quiet. Everyone had gathered around Breeze, whose hand clutched a piece of paper.

A letter had arrived.

Wren had only seen one book in her life, a copy of *Alice's Adventures in Wonderland* that her father had brought back after one of his conferences. She'd read it twenty-three times before her cousin Opal had destroyed it. Clepsits didn't care much for books. Some of them knew how to read, though—the first fathers and mothers, as well as a few others who helped with long-distance communications. Wren, as a future ambassador, had learned as well.

Letters, usually delivered by messenger pigeon but occasionally brought by a traveling clepsit, came rarely. They always resulted in some excitement and curiosity. Nevertheless, Wren didn't understand why the entire burrow had stopped everything to gape at the piece of paper. Even the hatchlings watched with interest. Breakfast grew cold on the table. No one spoke.

Breeze could read a little, though not as well as Wren, and it was unusual for her to handle correspondences.

"Who sent that?" Wren tried to take the letter,

which smelled faintly of rotten eggs, but her mother wouldn't let go. "What does it say?"

Breeze looked at Wren but said nothing. Her hands trembling, she gave the letter to Bronco. He read it, sat down, and read it again.

All eyes darted between Wren and the letter. A heaviness settled in the pit of her stomach. "What does it say?"

Bronco didn't answer her, either, so she turned to Iron. As first father of the clan, he read every letter that came in. He must have read it before giving it to Breeze.

"What does it say?" Wren repeated again.

"It's about Isaac," Iron said. "He's been killed. Your parents confessed to the crime."

Isaac jerked awake. At first he was aware only of the pain that coursed down his spine and legs: a horrible stinging and piercing sensation. Then memories of the voracans flooded his consciousness. They'd taken him. He had to escape.

He tried to run, but the voracans kept a tight grip on him.

No. The voracans weren't holding him. Not anymore. Something else secured him in place. Isaac forced himself to see past the pain. He needed to examine his surroundings.

A chair. A metal chair, cold and hard. The voracans had strapped him to it.

One voracan loomed over him, its body of black needles twisting in constant motion, while many more stood nearby.

"You must eat, eat," said the voracan.

Isaac looked at the bowl being offered to him. Despite his blurred vision, he determined that it contained some sort of meat. He hadn't eaten in ages, but the pain and exhaustion offset whatever hunger he felt. He could think about food after he slept some more.

"Eat," the voracan insisted. "Eat. Eat."

Isaac forced his eyes back open. "What is it?"

"Delicious vole. We can only eat the marrow, the marrow, but you can have the flesh."

The flesh in question was raw and bloody, with tufts of fur still attached. Had Isaac had any food in his stomach, he might have vomited it. "No."

"Would you prefer moles? Would you?"

"No. I'm not hungry. I just want to sleep." He closed his eyes.

The voracan prodded him with one of its many quills. "You must eat, eat."

"Why?" Isaac demanded. "Why do you care if I

eat, eat?" If they were going to hold him captive, the least they could do was let him rest. Or get him better food.

Why was he so tired? His entire body ached.

"You are weak, weak. You must build up your strength so that we can take more of your marrow, your marrow."

Isaac's exhausted mind struggled to make sense of this. "Marrow?"

"The marrow of your bones. Delicious, delicious."

Bone marrow. That was the stuff inside bones. Isaac didn't know exactly what it did, but he imagined it was something he needed. And the voracans thought it was delicious.

Isaac examined the chair he was sitting in. It looked like something pieced together from various odds and ends found in a garbage dump: mostly slabs of metal with sharp edges, but also plastic and wood, joined together with screws, bent nails, or even duct tape. There were tubes, too—lots of them, and each connected to a needle. The needles looked like what doctors would use to draw blood, only bigger.

"Is this chair supposed to take my bone marrow? So you can eat it?"

"Yes. Yes."

At the moment the needles dangled from the chair, limp and unused. Judging by the soreness in Isaac's arms and legs, though, he suspected that the needles had been used on him recently. "Why isn't it on?" he asked. Not that he was complaining.

"It's not working. The needles go into your bones, but little marrow comes out, little, little. None is stored, none, none. I must fix it. In the meantime, you must eat, eat."

"Not voles. Not moles, either."

"Yes. Yes," the voracan said, just before it scampered away on its limbs made of quills.

Isaac tried to stand, but he couldn't. Even without the restraints that secured him to the chair, he would've had a hard time moving. He was too tired, too sore. How much of his marrow had the chair taken before it stopped working? He wasn't sure, but he felt as though he could sleep forever.

Throughout Mrs. Read's phone call, Mr. Read paced back and forth between the living room and the kitchen. It annoyed her more than it should have. She knew he fidgeted when he was worried, and she didn't blame him for it. She was worried, too. But it was distracting, and this conversation was important.

When she hung up, he hurried over to her.

"Well?" he said. "What did they say?"

They were the people at the North American Headquarters for Clepsit-Human Relations. Mrs. Read had spoken to James Fife, whom she considered both a colleague and a friend. But the phone call had not gone well. "You might want to sit down for this."

Mr. Read sat on the sofa, then stood, then sat again. "I heard, on the phone, you said something about our not hurting Isaac. What were you talking about?"

Mrs. Read rubbed her temples. "There are many among the clepsits, and some among the humans, who believe we are responsible. The Snow Clan received a letter." She closed her eyes. "The letter claimed to be from us. It said that we could no longer tolerate Isaac, just as all humans can no longer tolerate clepsits."

"You have to tell them we didn't send that letter!"

"I did tell them that. Of course I told them that. You heard me tell them that!" Mrs. Read took a deep breath. Fighting wouldn't do anyone any good. "Some people—especially some of the clepsits—will be hard to convince."

"But why would we hurt Isaac? He's our son!" Mr. Read stood and resumed pacing. "And what would be the point of sending a letter like that and then denying it now? It doesn't make any sense."

"Human-clepsit relations have been so strained recently that many have been waiting for some type of catastrophe. And a lot of clepsits see humans as

76

rash and illogical, so some strange behavior on our part hardly gives them pause." She walked over to her husband and took his hand. "We need to pack."

"Why? Where are we going?"

"The North American Headquarters, where we can seek asylum. If you don't want to go there, we could go into hiding. We can't stay here. The clepsits know where we live, and without the protection of the headquarters, this place may not be safe for us."

"But what if Isaac returns?"

"That seems unlikely," Mrs. Read said.

Mr. Read stared at her. "How can you say that?"

"I don't mean that we won't get him back. I simply mean that he hasn't wandered off. He's been taken. We'll find him by figuring out who took him, and we may have better luck with that at the North American Headquarters. They have good resources."

"But they think we did it! Why would they help us if they think we're guilty? We should call the police." He reached for his cell phone.

Mrs. Read stopped him. "You know we can't involve human authorities in human-clepsit matters. It would be a huge breach of protocol—an act of hostility. In times like this, some might interpret it as an act of war. The police are a force of armed humans, after all. Clepsits don't see them as much different from an army."

"But we have to find Isaac."

"We will. But right now, we have to get away from here. It isn't safe."

So they packed a suitcase each, but before Mr. Read would agree to leave, he insisted on checking the house again, just in case they came across anything they had missed before. Then he searched the yard, the neighbor's yard, and the park where Isaac had played the afternoon before everything went horribly wrong, all for the second or third time. After taking several pictures for evidence, Mrs. Read changed Isaac's sheets. When they returned, she didn't want it to be to bloody bedding. Then she joined her husband outside.

"What's this?" he asked, holding up a long black spike he had found in the yard.

"I'm not sure." Mrs. Read took the item, which was about two feet long.

"It looks like some sort of quill," Mr. Read said. "Maybe from a porcupine?"

"It's too long," Mrs. Read said. "And it's pure black. Aren't porcupine quills black and beige? I think this is a voracan quill."

"A voracan? Isn't that the creature you had the conference about? The one that's been attacking people? Do you think it could have anything to do with Isaac?"

"Maybe," she said. "Probably not." Sniffing the quill, she thought she detected a whiff of sulfur—the same odor produced by the voracans' unusual digestion. And her husband was right. She had heard several reports of voracan activity during the conference. But the voracans had been coming up to the surface to eat, not to kidnap children and forge letters. "Listen, we can't bring it with us—airport security won't allow it in our carry-on luggage—but I'll tell the guys at headquarters. Maybe they'll know what's going on."

Mrs. Read put the quill back on the ground, but she snapped a picture for evidence. They went inside to grab their suitcases, and Mr. Read checked that the stove was off and emptied the trash. Then he disappeared, and after a few minutes of frantic searching, Mrs. Read found him in Isaac's room.

"Are you ready?" She tried to keep the impatience out of her voice, but she couldn't help looking over her shoulder. Some of the clepsits were angry. Furious. Who knew what they might do?

"Almost." Mr. Read finished writing a message on

a piece of paper and folded it into a neat square. "It's a note for Isaac, so he'll know to contact us at headquarters."

He put the piece of paper between Isaac's soccer trophy and the good luck charm Mrs. Read had given him. "If Isaac returns—*when* Isaac returns—he'll be sure to look here."

Following the arrival of the letter, no one ordered Wren to help with the cooking or collect wood for the fire. In fact, no one except Coney spoke to her much at all.

This didn't mean they ignored her. Aurora kept a suspicious eye on her. Her cousins whispered to each other, occasionally pointing at her. Her other brothers maintained a careful distance from her, and if she dared to come close, they flashed their claws in warning.

"It'll be okay," her mother promised, but there was sadness in her voice.

Having been kicked off the mat, Wren spent the nights on the cold, hard floor. She didn't need to worry about Opal's dream-fueled kicks—a definite bonus—but she still couldn't sleep, and not just because the stone floor made her body ache. When Kit wasn't snoring, she was whispering to Opal.

"I don't know why we're allowing her to stay in the clan."

"Father said we might be going to war," Opal replied. "Maybe we're keeping her so we can use her as a hostage later."

"I still don't think it's worth it, not after what her family did to ours. The ambassador program needs to be stopped. All it does is produce traitors and spies."

Wren's fingers curled into tight fists, her nails digging into her palms. How could Kit say that? Wren might not have always liked Kit, but she had always considered her a sister, a part of her family.

Because they *were* family. Wren belonged to the Snow Clan.

The next day, she set out to prove she belonged by contributing to the family as much as possible. After cleaning the furs and organizing the sewing supplies, she went to the cooking corner to see what else she could help with.

"Want me to do that?" Wren gestured to the dried vegetables that sat on her mother's cutting board.

"Yes, thank you." Breeze smiled, her eyes meeting Wren's, and for a second everything seemed normal. But then the smile faltered, and tears moistened her eyes. She opened her mouth to say something else.

Wren walked away before the words came out. She couldn't pretend that things were okay. Everything was messed up, and she had to find a way to fix it. Cooking and cleaning weren't enough, but perhaps her father would know what was.

Bronco had left the burrow to go fishing, even though they had plenty to eat already. In fact, they'd have to dry the surplus fish if they didn't want it to rot. But Wren knew it wasn't about food. He had gone fishing to escape the burrow. She wanted to respect his need for solitude—he had his son to grieve—but she had to talk to him.

She left the burrow. Everyone watched, but no one said anything—not to her anyway. She suspected the conversation began the second she was out of earshot. If she circled back, she could eavesdrop on them, but she didn't bother. She'd heard enough from Kit already.

The sun shone despite the cool breeze and the

storm clouds on the horizon. Although Wren hadn't seen a voracan in days, she carefully avoided the shadows.

Bronco sat at the edge of the river. His fingers gripped a fishing spear loosely as he stared off into space.

"Is it all right if I join you?" Wren asked, more than a little worried that he'd send her away.

He gave her a weak smile. "Of course."

Relieved, Wren sat down beside him.

A large fish swam by, but he made no effort to spear it. "You can't stay here."

Wren's forehead creased. She'd only just sat down. Why had he said she could join him if he wanted her gone already?

Then the real meaning of his words dawned on her. He wasn't talking about this particular spot by the river. He meant she couldn't stay in the forest. In the clan.

"It isn't safe," he continued. "I fear what my brother may do. I worry about what might happen to you if war starts."

Another fish swam past. Even when its head broke the surface of the water, Bronco made no move to spear it.

"Do you think my parents really . . . really . . ." She couldn't bring herself to say what, exactly, they had been accused of doing. "Really did it?"

"No. But that's what the letter says."

"Can I see it?"

He shook his head. It was a strange gesture, one the other clepsits didn't make. He'd picked it up from his time among the humans, along with nodding. "It doesn't say much. Just that they've killed Isaac, and that war must follow. Some, like Iron, are too willing to agree."

"Is it in their handwriting?"

"Not Faun's. She kept her clepsit name. She's always been so fond of clepsits. I've never seen her husband's writing, though, not that I can remember."

"I've been thinking. If they didn't send the letter, somebody else must have. Maybe it was the voracans. The letter smelled like rotten eggs. Remember? And when I was collecting firewood with Coney, I overheard the voracans say something about a clepsit boy. They must have meant Isaac."

"I noticed the smell, too. But why would the voracans do that? They're hardly more than animals. They don't send letters. They don't scheme." He shook his head, sighing. "No matter who wrote the letter, it seems that the conclusion is correct. Humans and clepsits cannot get along anymore. You need to go before things get worse."

He handed a small metal key to Wren. "This will let you into the rail station. I've packed a bag for you with food and a map. You'll find it in the entrance to the rails, hidden behind a loose rock in the wall. Hide from any clepsits you come across and go straight to the North American Headquarters. I wish I could go with you, but that would make me a traitor in Iron's eyes. He is urging war. I need to stay here so I can offer a counter opinion."

Another fish swam by. This time Bronco speared it.

***

Wren had thought about leaving the clan before. She'd fantasized about living in the human cities, where machines did all the work and no one teased her for being different. But as horrible as the burrow had become, it was the only home Wren had ever known. She wasn't eager to abandon it.

She decided to harvest some mushrooms before heading back inside. They still had some dried caps left from winter's stock, but everyone would enjoy some fresh specimens. The forest floor didn't offer very many, but she managed to find a few.

Footsteps fell behind her. Her muscles tensed and her stomach twisted as she realized where she stood. In her search for mushrooms, she'd ventured into shady areas. Now the voracans would attack.

Except voracans didn't have footsteps. They didn't have feet. Their spiky forms stretched out silently. So whose loud approach was she hearing?

Something sharp struck her shoulder. She turned around, half expecting to see a mess of black spines despite the heavy footsteps.

Her cousin Garnet snarled at her, his claws ready for a second strike.

Mercury and Cobalt stood behind him. "Get her!" they yelled. "Get the human!"

While Wren moved a hand to protect her face, Garnet clawed her stomach. Mercury and Cobalt moved in to pull her hair and bite her legs. Her fingers formed fists, which she swung at anything that came near her, but there were three of them and only one of her, and Iron had never allowed her to participate in the boys' fighting lessons.

She curled into a tight ball and waited for the attack to end.

"Stop it!"

Wren couldn't see the speaker, but she recognized the voice. It was Coney's.

"Stop it! Aurora said not to hurt her."

Wren had overheard the command from the previous day. Aurora's exact instructions had been not to hurt her *yet*. She didn't correct Coney. Her cousins eased off. After a couple of relatively soft scratches and blows, they wandered away.

Coney helped Wren up. "It's okay. They're gone."

It wasn't okay, though, and everyone knew it. Tears streamed down her face, and not just from the pain of so many cuts and bruises.

She was going to miss Coney most of all.

She was going to leave.

One of the voracans approached Isaac with a paper bag. "Eat, eat."

It might have been the voracan that had offered him food before. It looked and sounded the same, but Isaac had trouble telling the voracans apart.

Every single one of them looked like something out of a nightmare.

Each body consisted of a soft, roundish center—the closest thing the voracans had to a face—surrounded by quills. On the face were two eyelike orbs, short tendrils that occurred in irregular patterns, and a circular mouth. Instead of a tongue, there was a long, flexible quill that was actually more like a tube—a proboscis—used to suck marrow from victims. They must have had ears, but none that could be seen. They also appeared to lack a nose—luckily for them, considering the foul stench they exuded.

Many of the quills were large and sprouted directly from the face. Others were much smaller, some no larger than sewing needles, that sprang from small lumps of a fleshy substance attached to the ends of other quills. The result was a mess of quills resembling a tumbleweed, but sometimes the larger quills came together to form a sort of momentary limb—an arm here or a leg there, as needed. By moving the smaller quills, the voracans could manipulate their surroundings with more precision, though not as easily as they could have if they had hands.

With their quills stretched out, they reached a size of about three to four feet in diameter, but they could contract themselves into much smaller shapes, making it possible for them to funnel their hard yet flexible forms through narrow openings.

They all looked very similar—and equally horrific—but small variations among the voracans were starting to become apparent. Some had thicker quills than others, for example, and some had larger eyes, or whatever those black orbs were.

Isaac's eyes had adjusted somewhat to the darkness, and although he still couldn't see much more than shadows and shapes, he thought he recognized this voracan's thin quills and the slightly oval central mass that acted as its face. Its voice sounded softer, less grating, than the others; its movements were less jerky.

Whether or not the voracan was the same, the food was different. The aromas of salt and fat made Isaac's mouth water. He peeled away the paper wrappings to reveal that, instead of handing him another bowl of raw vole, the voracans had given him a hamburger.

Fast food was so much better than voles.

He ate it, all of it, down to the last sesame seed, even though it meant that the voracans were getting what they wanted. He drank the soda, too—what little remained, anyway. Most of it had leaked through several small punctures. Voracan quills weren't designed to hold disposable cups.

They were designed for piercing the bones of victims.

The food helped clear Isaac's mind. He managed to sit up a little straighter.

He was still strapped into the metal chair, but his arms had been freed so he could eat, and he wasn't nearly as sore as he had been. The area around him was small and dark, more like a hole in the ground than a room. A doorless entrance led to a corridor.

The only light came from a series of devices adhered to the dirt walls. They were like crude lamps, but dimmer, and the light they gave off was strange and reddish. They produced heat, too, more heat than light, and Isaac suspected that this was their main purpose. There were no wires that Isaac could see, but the lamps clearly used electricity. Maybe batteries powered them.

"Why do you need this machine?" he asked, noticing that the chair had a clunky back that could have been a container. "Are you trying to store my bone marrow?"

"Yes. Yes."

"Why?" Isaac recalled the voracans' boasts of planetary domination. "Is it part of your plan to conquer the surface?"

"Yes, yes. The surface will be ours, ours."

Isaac was about to ask more about the chair and how it worked, but he decided he'd really rather not think about it. "Why do you want to live up there?"

he asked instead. "You hate the daylight, don't you? You'll be miserable up on the surface, where it's sunny all the time."

"Not all the time. The sun disappears every night, every night. During the day, we will seek shelter, but the night will be ours, ours. The world will be ours, ours."

"It'll never work. The clepsits and the humans are too strong. United against you, they'll be even stronger." In fact, a rescue party must have been on its way. It probably would have gotten there already if Isaac hadn't kept the monsters lurking in his closet a secret. He'd meant to tell his mother as soon as she'd returned. Now it was too late.

Nevertheless, his parents would figure it out. They would find him. Any second now.

"Humans and clepsits will never unite, never, never. Already they speak of war."

"That's not true." Isaac's mother had called the conference tense, but she would have mentioned if war had been about to start. "Why would we fight each other?"

"You, you. The clepsits and humans will fight over you, and the voracans will conquer what is left."

Him? The clepsits and humans would go to war

over him? Isaac was the son of an ambassador. One day, he himself would serve as ambassador. His family helped secure peace; they didn't start wars. The very idea was ridiculous.

When his mother rescued him, he'd tell her everything. She'd know what to do. In the meantime, he just had to stay alive—something that would become more difficult once the voracans fixed their marrow-draining machine.

Coney's tail fell limp. "You can't leave. This is your home. Where would you go?"

"Father said I should go to the North American Headquarters. He's already packed a bag for me and stashed it in the rail station." She took a deep breath. If she delayed this at all, she might never work up the courage again. "I'm leaving today. Now."

Coney's eyes widened. "Now? Can't you wait until tomorrow?"

"Giving our cousins time to ambush me again?" She bit her lip. "No, I don't think so."

"But you have to say goodbye!"

Wren hesitated. She did want to say goodbye, especially to her mother. But Kit had told Opal that the ambassador program succeeded only in producing traitors and spies. With that belief, they might not let her leave. If her father had wanted to announce her departure to the rest of the clan, he would have done so. Instead, he'd set everything up so she could sneak away. That was what she had to do. "I'm saying goodbye to you. I think the Reads are innocent, and that they've been framed by the voracans. I have to find them. I have to help them prove that they didn't kill Isaac."

"I'll go with you." He started walking east, toward the rail station. They didn't talk, but Wren appreciated the company. After this, she wouldn't have any for a while.

"Here," Coney said, pointing.

A tree stump marked the entrance to the station. Once she saw it, she had no doubt it was the right one. The clepsit symbol representing the rails, which looked like two crisscrossed lines in a box, had been carved into the trunk. She would have walked right past it, though, if Coney hadn't drawn her attention to it.

Any of Wren's other siblings or cousins would

have teased her about the matter, but he pointed it out without comment, without showing off.

She really would miss him.

"How do we get in?" he asked.

"I'm not sure." Wren had heard about the rails many times, but she'd never actually been inside them. Not since she was an infant, anyway. The symbol marked the entrance, but how could they enter a solid stump? "Oh! The key."

She took out the key her father had given her. It slid into a thin slot in the stump. The top of the stump sprang up, revealing an opening.

Coney raced and Wren inched down the hole. After several yards, it opened into a space with enough room to stand and walk comfortably. The walls consisted of packed dirt lined with stones, all coated with a layer of special paint made by the aquatic clepsits of the tropics, which glowed in the dark. The resulting light, although dim, made vision possible.

It might not be enough to keep the voracans at bay. Wren just had to hope that they truly had lost interest in her, or that if they still wanted her, they wouldn't think to look for her in the rails.

Several carriages occupied one side of the room, where they remained in storage until required by a passenger. The rail system consisted of two rails: one going in a more-or-less southern direction, another going in a more-or-less northern direction. Both sloped down, using the force of gravity to propel the carriages forward.

Wren needed to go south, toward the headquarters, but first she needed to find the supplies her father had prepared for her. "Father hid a bag for me behind a loose rock. Help me look for it."

Coney sniffed out the bag almost immediately. It contained the promised supplies: dried fish and meat, dried vegetables, dried fruit, a canteen of water, and a map, as well as some clothes. There was a small wooden figurine, too, of two clepsits with their tails looped together in a symbol of good luck. An inscription carved into the bottom contained only two words: *Love, Father.*

"Are you okay?" Coney asked. "Is it your arm?"

Wren looked at her left arm, the same arm she'd used to shield herself from her cousins' attack, which had, as a result, suffered the brunt of the injury. Angry red lines marked where the claws had broken her flesh. It wasn't that bad, though, and she didn't understand Coney's sudden concern over it—until she realized she was crying.

She wiped her tears away. She didn't want Coney's memory of her to include her blubbering like a hatchling. "I'm okay."

"You're not bleeding much, but there's a lot of dirt in the cuts." Coney poured the water from the canteen over the scratches to clean them. Then he refilled the canteen with water from a drinking fountain in the corner of the room. "I guess we should move the carriage now."

It was heavy, but its wheels moved easily, and together they managed to get it onto the rail without difficulty. Wren climbed inside, wondering how she would say goodbye.

Coney climbed inside and sat next to her.

"What are you doing?"

Coney frowned. "I'm going with you. I already said I was."

"I thought you meant to the rail station to see me off. You can't go with me!"

"Why not?"

"Because . . ." Wren faltered. She didn't want to go alone, and she didn't want to leave Coney. He could help her. He could keep her company. The journey ahead of her seemed much less terrifying with him by her side. So why not? Why couldn't he join her?

For the same reason her father couldn't go with her. "Because our uncle and cousins already think I'm a traitor and a spy. If you come with me, they'll think the same of you."

"I don't care what they think."

"Well, you should." Wren could always return to human society, as foreign and strange as that sounded, but what would Coney do if Iron expelled him from the clan? "Besides, Father knows I'm leaving, but if you disappear, too, he won't know what happened. He'll be worried sick."

"But you'll be all alone."

Wren blinked away some tears. She had to sound strong or she'd never convince Coney. "Not for long. It's just a short trip on the rails. I'll be at the headquarters in no time. Father told me to go, but he didn't tell you to go. You're not allowed. You'll get in trouble."

Coney hesitated. He clearly didn't want that. "Are you sure you'll be okay?"

She wasn't. "Yes. I promise. Stay here and keep an eye on everyone. Help Father convince them not to go to war."

They hugged each other. Then Coney got out of the carriage, and there was nothing left for Wren to do but leave.

Isaac had stopped jumping at every sound. When a grating voice spoke or something in the distance thudded, he no longer lifted his head, his eyes wide and his heart thumping, to see if his rescue party had finally arrived. Even when the voracan came to tinker with the machine, he barely looked up. No one had come to save him, and he was beginning to wonder whether anyone ever would.

He couldn't keep waiting. He would have to rescue himself.

"I need to use the bathroom," Isaac said, although calling the portable toilet the voracans had brought in a bathroom seemed like a bit of a stretch. At least it had a door that closed. It looked just like the sort of thing he'd seen at construction sites and carnivals, and he suspected the voracans had stolen it from one of those places. He suspected they stole lots of stuff from humans, actually, including the scraps they used to build things and the hamburgers they fed him. They were monsters, after all, ones that didn't carry cash.

The voracan unfastened the metal clamps that secured Isaac to his chair. Its quills moved quickly, too fast for Isaac to determine how the lock worked. It looked like it required a small key, but Isaac hadn't seen one. Then the voracan returned to tinkering with the large, clunky back of the chair.

Isaac hesitated. Before, the voracans had prodded and shoved him. Now this voracan was practically ignoring him.

Not that this would make escape possible. One voracan had let its guard down, but there were others lurking nearby. And even if Isaac got past them, he wouldn't know how to navigate the dark corridors.

He'd find a way, though.

He stood, which felt good but kind of hurt, too. After a few stretches, he went into the portable toilet. He took his time, happy for a little privacy, though one cramped space wasn't much better than another. Eventually, he left.

The voracan was still working on the chair, trying to fix it. There were metal pieces attached to the ends of some of its quills. One was rough, another sharp, another large and flat. At first Isaac had assumed they were weapons, but now he suspected they were tools specially designed to fit on the voracans' quills. The metal-capped quills snaked through the many parts of the chair, sometimes twisting like a screwdriver and sometimes scraping like a chisel.

The tools might as well have been weapons.

As soon as it got the machine running, Isaac would be jabbed with needles, his bone marrow sucked out. He still didn't remember what marrow did exactly, but he was sure he needed his. He had to escape before the voracans drained him of it.

"I need to move," Isaac said.

"So move, move."

"There's not enough space here. I need room to walk around more. Otherwise I might get sick before you can test your chair on me." Of course the success of the chair wasn't really what worried him. He had ulterior motives—not an actual plan yet, but maybe he'd see something that would inspire one. And he really did need to move around more. Sitting so much was making him weak and listless.

The voracan moved in a motion not unlike standing, its quills arranging themselves in a form that was taller and straighter. "Follow me. Follow me."

The other voracans—there was often a cluster of them in the corridor—crowded around them. They pushed each other out of the way to get closer, and several of them got into scuffles that threatened to become brawls. Isaac felt their quills scrape against his arms, and he stayed close to his soft-voiced voracan guard.

They walked down a dark passageway. The strange red lamps that lit his room also illuminated the halls, though only dimly. Isaac's eyes had adjusted to the darkness, and he could see well enough.

The crowd of spectators thinned, and soon Isaac and the single guard were alone.

"Do you have a name?" Isaac asked.

"Yes. Yes."

"What is it?"

"Mine. Mine."

Isaac hesitated. "You're called *Mine*? Or your name is yours?"

"Yes. Yes." The passage forked. Something mechanical hummed to the left. The voracan went right. "This way."

Isaac still didn't understand whether or not the voracan was actually named Mine, but voracan naming conventions were low on his list of concerns. The strange humming interested him far more now. "What's down the other way?"

"My work." Mine, or whatever the voracan was called, jabbed Isaac with one of its long black quills. "Our victory, our victory."

Isaac quickened his pace. He wanted to investigate the humming, especially if the voracans believed it to be the key to their victory. He couldn't do it now, though, not when he was being watched so closely.

A group of thick-quilled voracans passed them in the corridor. They moved more slowly than some of the others. Perhaps the width of the quills indicated age, or maybe the bigger ones just couldn't match the speed of the smaller ones.

The corridor ended, but not before leading to a large room. Like all the other rooms Isaac had seen in the voracans' underground lair, there was no door—just a slightly irregular hole in the wall.

"What's in here?" Isaac asked, and he stepped inside without waiting for the answer.

The room was open and big, at least twenty feet wide and another twenty across, yet there was hardly any room to walk. Junk occupied every bit of space. Whole refrigerators and cars sat next to empty water bottles and soda cans. Batteries and lightbulbs filled cardboard boxes stacked one on top of the other in precarious towers. Piles of televisions, computers, and cell phones formed hills.

"Is this your trash?" Isaac asked.

"It is our treasure, our treasure."

Of course. The voracans didn't build computers and refrigerators. Humans did. Voracans took what they could so they could repurpose it into horrible, marrow-draining contraptions.

Isaac picked up an old snow globe and, when the voracan wasn't facing him, chucked it at a heap of electronics. "What's that over there?"

It was a cheap trick, but it was the best plan he could come up with. While Mine scanned the other side of the junk room, Isaac fled.

By nightfall the Snow Clan had begun to notice Wren's absence. They ate dinner without her, and although Breeze tried to set aside a little rabbit and a few vegetables, nothing was left after the boys had their fill.

"She probably got lost again," Aurora said. "I don't know how humans manage without a sense of direction. No wonder they're so cranky all the time." She handed a scrubber to Breeze. "Since she's not here to help, you'll have to do the pots."

Kit or Opal could have done it, or even one of the boys. Breeze took the scrubber without pointing this out. She didn't mind the cleaning, but she was worried about her daughter. "Has anyone seen her since this morning?"

Bronco said nothing.

Garnet, Cobalt, and Mercury snickered.

Coney shot his cousins an angry glance. "She left to collect fresh mushrooms for us."

"Poisonous mushrooms to kill us, no doubt." Aurora snorted. "Maybe she forgot they were poisonous and ate them herself. The girl never could resist food."

This was too much for Breeze. She threw down the scrubber. "This isn't a joke! We need to go look for her."

"You're right. We should find her," Aurora said. "But not to keep her safe. To keep us safe. Wren has known ties to the enemy. They're her parents after all. Who knows what treachery she's involved in at this very moment?"

"Treachery!" Bronco's tail shot straight up. "What disloyalty has little Wren ever been guilty of? If she left, it was to get away from the constant threat hanging over her here, not to collude with some enemy. We don't even know that the humans are the enemy."

One of the hatchling boys started crying. As Aurora picked him up, she said, "You read the letter with your own eyes, and it should have come as no surprise. Humans are vicious, violent creatures. Are you suggesting that someone who kills your son, your very own flesh and blood, is not the enemy?"

A million responses ran through Breeze's head, and none of them made any sense. How could she choose sides when it came to humans and clepsits? To Wren and Isaac? She picked up the scrubber again and started cleaning a pot. The scrubber slipped and, without noticing, she continued scouring with her fingers.

"I'm suggesting that letters can be forged," Bronco said. "I was raised by humans. Are you saying I'm vicious or violent? If you find her, what do you plan to do with her? Lock her up like a prisoner of war? Iron, as first father, you have a duty to protect her. She's a part of our clan."

Iron's expression matched his name: hard and cold. "No, she isn't. Not anymore."

Breeze put the pot down with a thud. "Then I'm not, either." She stormed out of the burrow and into the dark night. "Wren! Wren!"

Bronco followed close behind her. He held his wife, who was sobbing and shaking and still yelling for their daughter. Then he told her about the conversation he'd had with Wren earlier in the day. "Coney says he saw her off safely."

Breeze's weeping faded to silent tears. "Why didn't you tell me earlier?"

"I was afraid you'd chase after her, tell her not to go. I understand you want to protect her, but I don't think we can do that here. Not with Aurora convinced that humans are violent beasts that will kill us in our sleep. Not with Iron set on war."

"We should go after her," Breeze said. "Make sure she's all right."

"No," Bronco said, letting his tail entwine with hers. "She's strong, and she's well supplied. She'll make it to the headquarters, where she'll be safe. Besides, she's gotten too much of a head start. We'd never catch up. Even if we did, Iron would demand we bring her back here."

"So we'll disobey him." But even as she said it, she knew it could never happen. Iron was first father of the clan. Breeze would risk expulsion from the clan if it meant protecting her Wren, but she couldn't ask the same of her children. Coney. Colt. Taurus. Kit. If she defied Iron, her entire family would suffer.

Breeze and Bronco stayed outside for a while, just long enough to convince the others that they had searched for Wren, before returning to the burrow. The entire time, Breeze couldn't stop feeling that she'd failed as a mother to both Wren and Isaac.

The gentle slope meant that the carriage never went faster than a galloping deer, but it was still a much greater speed than Wren had ever experienced before. Her knuckles turned white as her fingers clutched the wooden sides of the carriage.

It came equipped with emergency brakes: a large bar that she could push down by using both her feet and all her strength. The brakes didn't cause the motorless vehicle to slow down, though, as Wren had hoped. Instead, the carriage came to a screeching halt, nearly ejecting Wren in the process. She did not try this a second time.

Her bag contained plenty of food, and she hadn't eaten in hours, but the constant motion made her stomach twist and flip. She couldn't read the map, either, not without getting a throbbing headache. There was nothing for her to do except sit back and wait for the ride to end.

Eventually, she fell asleep. The constant jerks kept her slumber light, and any particularly large bumps roused her, if only for a moment. Sometimes, in a state of only partial wakefulness, she saw shadows and thought that the voracans had launched another attack. Other times she heard a comforting voice and thought her mother had come for her, but it always proved a mere illusion. For better or worse, she was alone.

The slope became less and less steep until the rail lay in a perfectly horizontal line. The carriage slowed. Then the slope returned, but reversed this time, so that the rail climbed uphill. The carriage came to a gentle stop. She had reached the next station. A mile below it, anyway.

According to Iron, humans relied first on animals and later on motors for their transportation. Clepsits used simple tools powered by gravity and their own strength. As a result, they had no extra mouths to feed and no polluted skies to worry about. It seemed like a flawless method, and Wren had listened to many long lectures on its superiority, most of which were given by Aurora. Now, however, she had her doubts. Having stopped at the rail station, she could go no farther without traveling up to the surface.

There were elevators of a sort, but they were nothing like the automated elevators Aurora said lazy humans possessed. Wren pushed her carriage onto the large wooden platform and stood next to it. A complicated series of ropes attached the platform to a system of pulleys. She pulled down on these, and the platform rose. The pulleys did the majority of the work, but that still left plenty for her. Despite her frequent breaks, her arms soon ached, and sweat soaked her fur dress.

When she finally reached the top—though not quite the surface—she felt ready to collapse. She pushed her carriage off the platform in case someone else needed to use it. Then she dragged herself to the water fountain and, after pouring several canteens full of cool liquid onto her face, drank as much as she could.

She sat down where she was, even though the ground was wet, and opened her bag.

Her father had packed dried berries, one of Wren's favorites. She ate only a couple, setting the rest aside for later, and filled up on the dried rabbit instead.

This station was far larger than the one near her burrow. Rails radiated out in every direction, not just north and south. A symbol identified each line, and the ones Wren needed to follow to reach the head-quarters had been marked on her map. Even with her lousy sense of direction, she knew exactly which way to go.

She didn't need to go right now, though. The journey would be a long one, and the nap she'd managed in the carriage had been far from refreshing. She rummaged through the bag and removed the strange clothes her father had packed for her—large shoes with string crisscrossing up the front, a soft pink top, and pants made from some sort of blue cloth—very different from the fur and leather dresses she normally wore. Using these as a pillow, she settled into a corner, closed her eyes, and fell into a deep sleep.

A voice startled her awake. ". . . the human child."

The voracans had found her! She had to flee to the surface. Hopefully it would be day, and the shining sun would protect her. If not . . . well, hopefully it would be day. She had to hurry.

How fast did the voracans move? Could she out-run them?

"What about her parents, the ambassador and her husband?" came another voice, similar to the first but a little deeper. It didn't sound like a voracan, Wren realized. The air didn't smell like rotten eggs, either.

Two men were pushing a carriage off the platform. Their green skin identified them as tropical arboreal clepsits—definitely not spiny voracans. Both used their prehensile tails to hold their luggage.

"It's one thing to grant the child asylum, but the clepsit council can't be thinking of letting the murderers get away with their treachery."

Their carriage now back in its place, both men took large hooded robes from their bags and donned them. Their faces still showed, but between the hoods and the dim lighting, the greenness wasn't obvious. With their tails hidden under the bulky outfits, they carried their luggage in their gloved hands.

They walked toward the exit.

"Of course not. There's talk of setting up traps around the headquarters, in case they go there and then try to flee when they see what's happening. . . ."

They kept talking, but they were now too far away for Wren to hear.

There was a plan to trap her birth parents. There might be a plan to ensnare her, too. And these clepsits knew all about it.

Careful to make as little noise as possible, Wren gathered her belongings and followed the clepsits to the surface.

Isaac didn't make any attempt to flee into the junk room. Sure, there were lots of hiding places, but it was a dead end. Instead of getting himself cornered, he ran back the way they'd come. The voracan, Mine, chased after him.

Having spent so many hours strapped to a chair, his legs growing sore and stiff, he knew he didn't stand much of a chance. Though a surge of adrenaline propelled him forward, the lead the head start had given him began to shrink.

He came to the fork in the path. Glancing down

the passage that led to his chair, he saw a couple of voracans. Neither of them gave any indication of noticing him. They were too busy prodding each other. Something made a big cracking sound—it might have been a quill snapping in half.

Better one of their quills than one of Isaac's bones.

Without stopping, Isaac hurried past the fork and toward the humming he'd heard earlier.

The noise grew louder with each step. It drowned out the thud of his footsteps and the huffing of his breath.

A hole in the dirt wall opened on one side of the corridor. It led to a room, the source of the humming. Still running, Isaac entered.

The room seemed to stretch on for almost a mile, much bigger than even the junk room, though the ceiling wasn't especially high, only about nine feet or so. Isaac had never before seen a room so large, other than images of enormous warehouses in movies or on television. And it was like a warehouse, a sort of storage space for machines. There were different types, each one pieced together from mismatched odds and ends. Some of them were turned on, humming loudly.

Most of the machines were bulky vehicles that

resembled tanks. Some had massive drills attached to the top. These must have been used to tunnel through the voracans' underground world. The rest were armed with various cannons, blades, or other weapons. Sitting inside one of these, a voracan could wage war at any time, shielded from the daylight.

In addition to the tanks, there was a type of machine now very familiar to Isaac. An uncomfortable metal seat. An equally cold and rigid back. Tangles of tubes ending in large needles. Metal clamps to keep the occupant in place.

His chair.

Hundreds of these marrow-collecting machines filled the room. The chair that Isaac sat in was only a prototype.

Upon closer inspection, it became clear that the tubes weren't connected to anything. The chairs didn't work—yet. Mine was still figuring out the design. Once Isaac's chair was working, the others would be fixed as well, new victims strapped inside.

Isaac wanted to destroy them, but they were large and numerous, and he was being followed. He hid behind them instead.

The voracan entered.

Isaac's breathing was heavy and loud, but nothing

compared to the constant humming of the machines. The voracan could not hear him. The red lamps that clung to the walls gave off only dim light, and the bulky chairs hid Isaac well. The voracan could not see him, either. He was safe.

Isaac tiptoed toward the tanks.

The voracan paused for a moment, as if scanning the room. Then it moved toward Isaac.

A coincidence. The voracan couldn't know where Isaac hid. Crouching down low, and careful to keep a chair between him and the voracan at all times, Isaac scooted to a new hiding spot.

The voracan changed its course immediately. Once again, it was headed straight for Isaac.

Isaac went left, then right, then left again, zigzagging between the chairs, and the voracan mirrored his every movement. Although Isaac didn't understand how, the voracan obviously saw him.

Hiding was no longer an option. That left running. Again.

He jumped up and dashed toward the nearest tank, about twenty yards away. His tail swung up to help his balance, and his hands hit the floor with each stride, which resembled a cheetah's gait more than a human's. He'd had almost no practice running like this, but instinct took over, and he achieved great speed despite having to dart around the many chairs in his way.

If he hadn't been fleeing for his life, it would have been amazingly fun.

Unable to slow down quickly enough, his body slammed against the tank. The collision jolted his bones and bruised his skin, but he didn't hesitate. His hands pushed and pulled at the rough and ragged edges of the machine. His fingers searched for a handle, a latch, anything that might provide entry. He found nothing.

Pain shot through his arms.

Looking down, he saw that two large black spikes had pierced his flesh—one in each arm. He tried to wriggle free, but each attempt sent pain radiating through his body. The voracan had him pinned against the side of the tank.

"You are brave, brave," Mine said. "Braver than is good for you. If the others had caught you, they would have done worse, worse."

The voracan led Isaac back to his room, back to his chair.

Coney tried to stay out of the way. In particular, he tried to stay out of Aurora and Iron's way.

"Maybe I should stay here," Aurora said, prying one of her hatchlings from the sewing supplies he'd gotten into. "You can't possibly be up to the task of running this place on your own."

Ether smiled politely, though her tail bristled slightly. "Don't be silly. Oak and I will be fine, and if we need any help, we can always go to one of the neighboring burrows. River has already offered to watch the hatchlings. Besides, your eldest children are mature enough to do a lot of the work on their own. Breeze's, too."

Aurora scowled. "I still don't understand why Breeze is going with us. She doesn't represent the clan, and she's not an ambassador."

"She's probably just eager to see the outside world." Ether yanked her tail from a hatchling's mouth. "I can understand the appeal."

Coney kept his mouth shut despite knowing full well that Ether had drawn the wrong conclusion about his mother. Like most members of the clan, Breeze had never left the forest before. But she'd never expressed any interest in a journey, either—not until now.

Something had made her change her mind, and it wasn't an interest in seeing some polluted city or boxy gray building. She wanted to make sure Wren reached her destination safely—just like Coney.

Coney went to his parents' sleeping room, a small and cozy space, where he found his mother packing her clothes into a leather bag.

"Your father says I won't be able to wear these fur dresses in the cities," she said, "but I don't have anything else."

"I want to go with you," Coney said.

Breeze smiled. "I know. I figured it out after the tenth or eleventh time you mentioned it."

"Father said I could go. He said I might be able to help."

"He did not. You're a terrible liar. Your ears always twitch."

Coney put his hands over his ears, which were still twitching a little. "Okay, maybe he didn't actually say it aloud, but he must have been thinking it. Or at least he should have been. I'm worried about Wren, too. She's my sister."

Breeze knelt down beside him. "I know, but we don't know what the situation will be like. I want you here, where you're safe."

But Coney wouldn't be dissuaded from helping his sister, not a second time. He never should have let Wren convince him to stay behind. "I have as much a right to be there as you. Nobody summoned you, either."

In fact, no one had requested Bronco's presence, either. The letter had asked only for the representatives of the clan, the first father and mother, without any mention of the North American ambassador. Bronco had raged at the oversight, his tail standing straight up and his voice rising until it was loud enough to scare off any wild animals within a mile radius.

It was a glaring error, he concluded, and he'd go whether or not he'd been asked. Breeze insisted on going, too.

Although no one said it, the headquarters never made mistakes. If they had omitted Bronco's summons, they had done it on purpose. They hadn't requested the ambassador because they didn't plan to negotiate with humans any longer.

"That's beside the point," Breeze said. "But I'm your mother, and I'm saying you can't come, so that's that."

"Fine," Coney said, careful to cover his ears. "I'm going to collect more firewood."

Instead, he went to the rail station. If his parents wouldn't let him accompany them, he would go alone.

His parents would be furious when they discovered his departure. Aurora would scold him. Iron might banish him. The knowledge turned his stomach to a heavy lump.

His mother was right about him being a bad liar. It was because he didn't get much practice at it. He didn't have a lot of experience getting into trouble, either. It made him nervous.

But not as nervous as he got thinking about Wren, out there and alone, most of her clan having turned on her. He would get into trouble later. Wren was in trouble now.

Wren maintained a safe distance between herself and the green clepsits. They had mentioned her, the human girl. For all she knew, they were looking for her, eager to turn her in for some imagined act of treason. She couldn't let herself get caught.

But she needed to know what they knew. If traps awaited her at the headquarters, she had to find somewhere else to go.

She also needed to learn what was going to happen to the Reads. Whether there was anything she could do to help them. Because her human parents—her birth parents—were innocent. They had to be. The voracans hadn't been interested only in Wren. They mentioned a clepsit boy—in hindsight it was obvious they meant Isaac. And the letter had smelled like rotten eggs: a clear sign the voracans had sent it. The more Wren thought about it, the more convinced she became.

Everyone else could have seen it, too, if only clepsits weren't so convinced that humans were violent and untrustworthy.

The green clepsits spoke to each other. Wren only caught a couple of words here and there, like "dinner" and "sleep." Nothing important. She stayed back as they exited the clepsit rail station.

After a brief pause, she followed.

She had never seen a human city before, not even in pictures. The sooty, overcrowded images that filled her dreams had been based on Iron's stories and Aurora's rants, but they were nothing like the gleaming city that surrounded her now.

Tall buildings jutted up from the ground to the sky. Wide paths, strangely smooth and hard, formed a series of straight lines and right angles that stretched on as far as she could see. People walked on the outer gray parts of the path. Carriages, much larger than the one she'd ridden in, zoomed past her on the inner black part of this path. According to Aurora, the unseen motors that powered these carriages also polluted the air. Wren didn't notice the thick black smog she'd been warned about, but the air did smell different from what she was used to.

Down in the clepsit rails, she'd lost track of time. Now she could see that it was night, though one very unlike what she'd grown used to. Things that resembled trees in their basic shape, but with smooth gray trunks and no leaves, lined the paths in neat rows. At the top of each one hung a bright light, like a miniature sun. As a result, Wren, whose night vision had never matched that of her clepsit family, could see quite well.

There were other lights, too, streaming out of buildings and radiating from signs. Some of them flashed words and pictures in colors brighter than spring flowers.

The door she'd exited from belonged to a plain building crammed between two other plain buildings. The number 377 had been painted above the door, and the symbol for the clepsit rails had been carved into it. It locked shut behind her.

A woman—a human woman, for they were all human here—frowned at Wren. "You all right? Do you need help?"

"Yes. I mean no. I'm fine." Others had gathered around them. Wren couldn't understand why she should attract so much attention. She was a human in a human society. Shouldn't she fit in for once?

Or did she not fit in anywhere?

Perhaps her fur dress made her stand out, she realized. No one else wore fur, and only a few people wore leather. Their clothes were tight, well tailored, and reminded Wren of the outfit her father had packed for her. He had packed it for a reason, of course. She should have put it on, but she'd been in such a hurry that the idea hadn't occurred to her until now.

"Where are your parents?" the woman asked. Her lips were bright red. Although Wren didn't know all the physical variations of her species, she suspected that the color was not natural. It looked too thick, too shiny, like it had been painted on.

Why would she paint her face?

Wren scanned the city block for the green clepsits. She spotted them on the other side of the path. "They're right there. I'd better catch up!"

She ran into the black part of the path. One of the

motored carriages speeding past screeched to a halt. Making a noise like that of an irritated goose, it went around her. She hurried to the other side.

The arboreal clepsits attracted a few curious glances, but their hoods kept their green faces more or less concealed. No one stopped to see whether they needed help. After a while, they entered a squat building. The brightly lit interior was filled with tables, only a few of which were occupied by humans. Everyone was eating, but no one was eating the same food. The kitchen must have been enormous to produce such variety.

The two clepsits approached a woman standing behind a tall, narrow counter. They were saying something, but Wren couldn't hear what. She edged closer.

"Yes, just the two of us," the taller of the two clepsits said. "A corner booth, please."

"You betcha." The woman tilted her head as she tried to get a better look under their hoods. "What's with the makeup?"

"Stage makeup for a play down the street," the shorter clepsit said.

"Taking it off between performances is too much work," the taller one added.

The woman nodded. "What's the play about?"

"Martians," the shorter one said.

"Mutants," said the taller one at the same time. Then he clarified, "Mutants from Mars. But certainly nothing for humans to worry about."

The woman led the clepsits to an empty table near the back of the building. They spoke in hushed tones, so Wren had to get very close to hear them. To avoid being seen, she ducked under an empty table.

"So what were you saying about these traps at headquarters?" the shorter clepsit asked.

"Well, the ambassador and her husband have already abandoned their house in Salmon City, so it's assumed they're heading to headquarters for asylum. We want to make sure they don't change their minds."

"What about their claim that the boy is still alive? They're saying they didn't send the letter, right? They think Isaac was taken, not killed, and that the kidnappers sent the letter to frame them. Is anybody planning to launch a search mission for the boy?"

The taller clepsit laughed. Something under his cloak made a bulge around his shoulders—his tail was sticking up. "Don't tell me you believe that story. Why would anyone kidnap the boy?"

A woman, older than the one who had seated them, put a basket of food on the table. She wrinkled her forehead at the two clepsits, both of whom still wore their hoods. "Is your skin green?"

"It's makeup for a play," the taller clepsit explained.

"Ah. What can I get you two to drink?"

"Two waters, no lemon," the shorter clepsit said as he took some food from the basket. When she left, he said, "Humans kidnap children all the time. Maybe someone realized the boy was special and thought they could get money for him."

"Then it's still the humans' fault. Most likely, though, the Reads killed the boy. Being arrogant, shortsighted humans, they decided to boast about it in that letter, but then they thought better of it. Now they're hoping a search party will distract the clepsits from what's really going on: the war humans are planning. They must not think we're too bright if they expect us to fall for it—no offense to you."

"You don't really think there will be a war, do you?"

"Humans have attacked clepsits before," the taller clepsit said. "There's no reason to think they won't again. This time, though, I hear clepsits are planning to fight back."

Wren bit her lower lip as she processed this information.

The Reads thought Isaac was still alive.

Wren already suspected that the letter was fake. The Reads hadn't killed Isaac. The voracans had. But she had never stopped to question whether Isaac was actually dead. If she could find Isaac, she could prove the Reads' innocence. She could show everyone that humans weren't the horrible creatures Aurora always said they were.

The woman returned with two cups of water.

"Hey! Whatcha doing under there?" She was smiling at Wren. "Are you looking for something?"

"No. I'm fine," Wren whispered, hoping the woman would go away.

That didn't happen. After putting down the two cups, the woman extended a hand to help Wren up. "What an interesting dress! Are you in the play, too?"

Everyone in the building was staring at Wren—including the clepsits.

Did they recognize her? She was a human in a human city, but she was wearing a clepsit dress. And perhaps they had seen a description of her, of her bright red hair and angular face.

The two clepsits stood.

Pushing her way past the woman, Wren ran outside.

Other than the biannual moves, Mr. Read had never traveled much. When Mrs. Read left town on clepsit business, he stayed home with Isaac. He used to envy his wife's trips, but he was beginning to think he'd gotten the better end of the deal.

He'd spent the day scrambling from terminal to terminal, rushing only to wait when the plane was delayed. "I don't understand why we had a layover in Miami, Florida. The headquarters aren't that far from Salmon City."

Mrs. Read glanced over her shoulder, a nervous gesture that was quickly becoming a habit. "It was cheaper."

Mr. Read suspected his wife was lying. He'd seen the price of the tickets; there was no way they'd saved money. She'd chosen not to fly direct for entirely different reasons.

A scarf covered Mrs. Read's short hair. Sunglasses shielded her eyes. She'd purchased both of these items during the layover in Miami. She looked over her shoulder again.

After getting off the plane, they boarded a train. Then they got in a taxi.

"Drive around the block, will you?" Mrs. Read asked.

The taxi driver shrugged. "It's your money." He drove around once. Then, following Mrs. Read's instructions, he drove around again.

"What exactly are you looking for?" Mr. Read asked. He'd been staring out the window, but all he saw was an average city block. Duller than average, actually. Even the bushes were square.

"Anything unusual." She raised her voice to address the taxi driver. "Okay, you can stop now."

After paying the driver and collecting their bags from the trunk, they entered the headquarters. It was a plain gray building, a boxy structure that verged on ugliness, the type of place people would forget immediately after viewing. The lobby looked like it belonged to some mundane office, with gray carpet, a large gray desk, gray chairs, and gray tables. A couple of bouquets of fake flowers had been put out in a feeble attempt to liven the place up.

Two men stood near the door. A middle-aged woman worked behind the large desk. All three were human. Mr. Read searched for signs that this was indeed the North American Headquarters for Clepsit-Human Relations, but other than his wife leading him there, he found none.

The receptionist gestured for the Reads to wait while she made a quick phone call. Her expression was serious, with just a touch of fear in her eyes. She put down the phone and flashed a fake smile. "Faun Read, you're here. We have a room ready for you. Our security officers will escort you."

She signaled for the two men, who accompanied the Reads to the elevator. One of them had blond hair and a jutting chin, the other a bald head and enormous hands. Neither of them spoke.

The bald security officer used his large fingers to press the button for floor six.

Mr. Read looked back and forth between the two

security officers. "How long have you been working here?"

"That's classified," the blond one said. The other one grunted.

"Oh, sorry." Mr. Read forced his smile bigger and brighter. "Do you like working here?"

"That's classified," the blond one repeated. The other one grunted again.

Mr. Read wondered whether they were messing with him. It hardly seemed like the time for levity, though, and they didn't strike him as the type to joke around. But maybe that was what made it funny.

He wished he were at home. "Have you heard anything about Isaac?"

The blond man raised his eyebrows. "Only that he's dead and you're responsible."

Apparently, that wasn't classified.

The elevator stopped at floor six. After checking the hall, the security officers motioned Mr. and Mrs. Read out. After checking the hall for herself, Mrs. Read followed them.

They took out a key and opened a door to what looked like a normal extended-stay hotel room, complete with a bed, a television, a bathroom, and a kitchenette. There were many of these rooms at the headquarters, Mrs. Read had informed him, since some of the more unusual-looking guests couldn't very well go to one of the nearby hotels.

"You've been granted asylum," the blond security officer said. "So as long as you don't leave the premises, we guarantee your absolute safety. Do not tell anyone which room you're staying in. Do not answer the door without looking through the peephole and verifying that it is one of us. Do not leave your room for any reason."

Mr. Read laughed nervously. "If you guarantee our absolute safety, why is all that necessary?"

The two security officers ignored Mr. Read, as did his wife. "We understand," she said. "When will the chief advisors be available for meetings?"

"Later this evening," the blond one answered. The bald one grunted. Both security officers turned around and left.

"Hey," Mr. Read shouted when they were halfway out the door. "Don't we get a key?"

Without answering, they closed the door behind them.

"If we're not allowed to leave," Mrs. Read explained, "we don't need one."

B ack in his chair, Isaac sat still while Mine dealt with his injured arms. The water it used looked clean, but maybe not sterile. It was probably the same water it brought Isaac to drink between meals of fast-food hamburgers and soda, which never tasted quite right. The bandages the voracan used to stop the bleeding were nothing more than old rags. Its quills scraped his skin as it wrapped the bandages around his arm.

Isaac used to get annoyed when his father duti-fully disinfected every tiny cut and scrape with sting-ing liquids and ointments. Now, faced with the threat of gangrene and sepsis, he missed his father's careful eye.

He missed his parents. Why hadn't they come for him yet?

"Your weapons are nothing compared to what the humans have," Isaac said. "They have missiles. Nuclear bombs. Poisonous gases. You only have one small arsenal." Though admittedly not that small.

"No, no. We have more, more. Stockpiles kept all over the world, and growing every day. And we have ourselves." It flashed its sharp proboscis. "We are so many, so many, and so hungry."

Oh. But humans still had better weapons. Although now that Isaac thought about it, he realized that humans had never had to fight an enemy that came from below. Their air strikes would prove useless. And even without any weapons, the voracans were plenty threatening, plenty frightening.

The humans could defeat the voracans. Probably. Eventually. But it would be better for everyone if they didn't have to.

"Why don't you just eat animals?" Isaac asked. "They have bone marrow, too."

"We do. We do. We eat moles and voles, whatever we can find underground. But the bones are so small, so small. It is not enough, so we must go up to the surface, where there is so much food, so much."

"Okay, but why eat humans and clepsits? It would be a lot easier to farm cows and pigs."

"No, no. Humans would not let us. They see us, they kill us. Before, we hid. Now we will conquer. We will. We will."

"No. You won't. My parents are looking for me. When they find you, they'll stop you."

"They are not looking," Mine said. "They are not. They are not. They think you are dead. And the clepsits think they killed you. Humans and clepsits will go to war. We will take what is left. That is the plan, the plan."

Isaac assured himself that this couldn't be true. Nobody would ever believe his parents had hurt him, and they would never give up looking for him.

Although they hadn't found him yet. Which wasn't very encouraging.

He decided to focus on something else—something that might help him plan how to escape the voracans on his own. "How were you able to find me so easily?" he asked.

"I saw you, saw, saw. I felt you, felt, felt."

"But I was hiding behind a machine. How could

you see me? And you weren't touching me. How could you feel me?"

"How can you see smell without touching? It is easy, easy."

Smelling was different from touching. But when he thought about it, Isaac supposed he felt temperature without touching anything. "What exactly do you see and feel?"

"Why do you want to know? Why? Why?"

"I'm curious," Isaac said, trying to sound casual—like he wasn't gathering information to aid his escape. He would have shrugged if his arms weren't injured and strapped down. "Bored, too. And if voracans are going to be the next rulers of the planet, I think I should know a little about you."

"You lie, lie. You want to know more about us so you can defeat us."

"So? What do you think I'm going to do?" Isaac moved his arms as far as he could, which was less than an inch. The resulting pain made him wince. "I'm stuck here, remember. My escape effort didn't go very well."

"Yes, yes." The voracan ran its quills along the metal clamps of the chair. "I see your heat. I feel your energy. It radiates off you, radiates, radiates."

Of course. The voracans lived underground. For now, anyway. Their eyes worked well enough for them to detect—and be sensitive to—light, but they needed other ways of navigating their dark underground world.

He remembered that the strange red lamps that dotted the tunnels also emitted heat. They were infrared lamps, he realized, and the voracans probably sensed the warmth they produced.

The voracans might sense electricity, too, including the small amounts living creatures produced. That could be the energy Mine had been talking about, and it would explain how Mine had found Isaac so easily.

Voracans wouldn't be the only species with this ability. Isaac's homeschooling classes had always stressed biology and ecology—subjects he'd need as a future ambassador—and he'd studied electroreception. He knew that some animals, like sharks, could sense electromagnetic fields. He'd even found it pretty cool back when it hadn't affected him. Now he'd rather face a hammerhead than a voracan.

The voracans wanted to take over the surface world. They wanted to conquer the clepsits and the humans, and they planned to turn the survivors into farm animals. Isaac had thought it impossible, but he'd also thought he'd have been rescued swiftly. He'd been wrong.

The voracans had an entire armada. Multiple ones.

With enough time, Isaac could figure out how to operate the voracans' machines. Once he'd done that, he could use them to escape. He could warn both humans and clepsits.

He needed to get back to that room. But that meant getting out of the chair again. It meant sneaking past enemies with both heat vision and electroreception to track him.

"If you are bored," the voracan said, "I can find you a game, a game."

What kind of a game would voracans play? Isaac didn't want to know, but he forced himself to nod. "I'd like that."

He would behave like a model prisoner. He would bide his time until the voracans relaxed their guard again. Then, when the opportunity struck, he would be ready.

The voracans had not won yet.

W ren ran for several minutes before realizing that no one was chasing her. She ran several more minutes before slowing down, just in case.

Green signs at every intersection labeled the paths with numbers: FIRST, SECOND, THIRD, and so on. She remembered that the door leading to the rail station had a number above it, too. Aurora always criticized humans for their poor sense of direction. Wren, hardly capable of finding the burrow on her own, couldn't really disagree. Yet humans managed to find their way around sprawling cities. The numbers must have been how they did it.

She was on Second now. If she reversed her course and stayed on Second, she would return to the building where the arboreal clepsits had been. That would bring her close to the rail station, but she'd have to make a left turn to get there. Or was it a right turn? Or two left turns?

Stupid human lack of direction! If Coney had been there, he could've led them back to the rail station instinctively.

If Coney had been there, she wouldn't have been alone. Before, she'd dreamed of an easy life among humans, where she'd finally fit in, but her current reality was nothing like her fantasies. She longed for her burrow, small and cramped though it was. At least there, she'd had family. She'd been loved, not by everyone, but by some. In the human city, she felt tiny. Insignificant. Lost.

She *was* lost.

She couldn't simply retrace her steps, either, even if she did manage to remember the way. The arboreal clepsits might see her if she tried that. She had to find another route to the station.

The paths seemed to form a grid of straight lines. If she took one of the parallel paths back, she should end up close to the right place. Probably. The map her father gave her didn't include any details for the human cities that lay above the rail stations. He hadn't meant for her to venture there.

Wren had never liked the dark. Her siblings and cousins had better night vision than she did, and some of them took advantage of this to sneak up on her and scare her. But she didn't like the harsh light of the human city, either. It seemed unnatural.

If she didn't fit into human society and the clepsits no longer accepted her, where did she belong?

No. This was no time for self-pity. She had a task to complete. She had people to save.

She walked over to one of the parallel paths, this one labeled THIRD, and hoped it would get her close enough to where she needed to go.

People kept staring at her. If she could put on the clothes in her bag, she knew she would attract less attention, but she didn't have anywhere to change. Careful not to look anyone in the eye, she tried to keep her pace fast and her head high, as if she knew exactly where she was going. She counted the places where the paths intersected. She'd passed six such intersections already. But how many had she passed while following the arboreal clepsits? And how many more had she passed running away from them? She should have been counting all along.

She went one more intersection before returning to Second. Nothing on the path looked familiar. Was that because she'd gone too far, or because she hadn't gone far enough? She kept walking. Still nothing she recognized.

After a while, the clusters of people on the paths began to thin, and the motored carriages passed less frequently. Some of the lights in the buildings flicked off.

Something squeaked. Looking over her shoulder, Wren saw the source of the sound: a cart full of blankets and bags being pushed by an old woman. Wren walked faster. The squeaking persisted, and every time Wren glanced back, the old woman was still there, smiling back at her with a toothless mouth. It might have been coincidence—perhaps that woman simply happened to be traveling in the same direction—but Wren turned the next corner just in case.

The squeaks made by the cart did not grow fainter. Wren made another turn, and behind her, the woman did the same.

Wren now knew for certain that she was being followed.

With equal conviction, she also knew that she was totally and completely lost.

A black-and-white motored carriage pulled over next to Wren. The large man inside spoke to her. "It's a little late for a girl your age to be wandering the streets, don'tcha think? And on such a cold night. Where are your parents?"

Wren hesitated. She couldn't tell him the truth, but she could use his help. The old woman, who had slinked off into the shadows at the motored carriage's approach, still watched from a distance. "They're waiting for me at door three-seven-seven. Do you know where that is?"

"You mean address three seventy-seven? Which street?"

"I don't remember. It's around here, though." Unless she had walked farther than she'd realized. Given the soreness of her feet, that was a strong possibility.

He looked at her dress. "I can't place your accent. Where are you from?"

"North of here."

"You mean Canada?" he asked.

"Yes," she said, although she had no idea what "Canada" meant. Maybe it was the human word for the forest she was from. "Can you help me find door—address—three-seven-seven?"

"Yeah, sure. Why don't you come with me to the station, and we can get everything figured out there? Maybe we can even find some hot chocolate for you. Now how does that sound?"

Not good, and not only because Wren had never heard of hot chocolate. She didn't know what station he was talking about, but since he wasn't a clepsit, she had to assume it wasn't the rail station. Going with him would mean going in the wrong direction.

She didn't know if she could refuse, though. The man was getting out of his black-and-white carriage, which had writing Wren didn't understand all over it. POLICE. She didn't know that word. IN CASE OF EMERGENCY CALL 911. Was she just supposed to scream the numbers? Regardless of how it worked, the carriage appeared to be special. Official.

Badges and patches decorated the man's crisp black outfit, also very official-looking. He must've been some sort of first father, like Iron. Disobeying him would land Wren in trouble.

She racked her brain for a good excuse not to go with him. But what constituted a good excuse in human society? "Sorry, I can't—"

"Officer Pete!" The old woman with the squeaky cart ran toward them. "You got to help, Officer Pete!"

The man tore his gaze away from Wren to look at the old woman, who was jumping up and down and flailing her arms—quite a show for a woman of her age. "Calm down, Mary. What's the problem?"

"There's a mad man!" she screamed, anything but calm. "You got to hurry. He's threatening to hurt people!"

Did this sort of thing happen often in human society? If so, maybe Aurora had been right about the species. They really were violent and dangerous.

Although Wren hoped everyone was okay, she didn't stick around to find out. She had never been able to move as quietly as her siblings or cousins, but the unnaturally smooth ground didn't have any leaves to crunch or twigs to snap, and in her soft leather shoes, she hardly made any noise. While the man and woman spoke, she sneaked away.

After turning one corner, then another, she was more lost than ever, but at least she'd escaped the humans and avoided the mad man.

Or not. A series of squeaks signaled the old woman's approach. "You got a tail?" she asked.

"N-no," Wren said.

"Don't worry none about that mad man. That was a slight fabrication on my part. I told Officer Pete you went off in the other direction, too. Thought he might be giving you a hard time."

"Thanks," Wren said, still confused about what had happened and concerned about the mention of a tail. It was probably best if she moved on. She continued walking down the path.

The old woman followed. "I lived in lots of places, from the Deep South to New England—none of them half as strange as this town. I see all sorts come through here. People with green skin, white fur, or blue fins, wearing strange vestments like that frock you got on. Most of them got tails, though they try to keep them under wraps. I follow them sometimes; keep an eye on them. I know where that X building of yours is, though I ain't never worked up the nerve to enter it myself."

Ex-building? What did she mean *ex-building*? The best Wren could figure was that it had to be some sort of former building, though she couldn't imagine what it was now. And she had no idea why the woman thought it belonged to her.

Half of what came out of the woman's mouth was nonsense, and the other half hinted at knowledge of clepsit secrets. Wren decided to get away before the woman's blabbering landed both of them in trouble.

People were supposed to walk on the outer gray paths, not the inner black part where carriages sped along. That much was obvious to even the most casual observer. But there were no carriages around at the moment, and Wren didn't see the harm in breaking the rules just this once. Anything to get away from the woman.

She stepped into the black path.

"You sure are lost! This way." The woman tugged at Wren's elbow. "Tell me what that *X* stands for. Is it a Roman numeral? And why is it stretched out all funny like that?"

"I don't know what you're talking—" Wren stopped. She *did* know what the woman was talking about. Not *ex-building*. *X building*. The building with the rail symbol, which looked like a flattened *X* in a box, on the door. The building labeled 377. The one she so desperately needed to find. "You know where it is?"

"That's what I been trying to tell you! Come along now, before Officer Pete finds us. He's well meaning, he is, but he don't know about your kind."

With the old woman and her squeaky cart, they made their way to the plain gray building that housed the rail station.

"You going to tell me what this place is?" the woman asked, grinning toothlessly.

Wren hesitated. The old woman was helping her, and she seemed nice, but everything about clepsits had to be kept secret from humans. Otherwise, Aurora warned, humans would attack clepsits, the way they had in the past.

Maybe Aurora was wrong, but it wasn't a risk Wren could take, especially when her family was already being accused of treachery. "I can't. I'm sorry."

"That's all right. Don't worry your pretty little red head about it. I'd probably just forget it anyway." She tapped her head. "Nothing stays in here. Now you better hurry along. Officer Pete could come back any second, and he'd haul you off before you could say social services."

Why would Wren say that?

She didn't bother asking. She thanked the old woman again. Using her key, she opened the door and stepped inside. Before venturing far from the door, she scanned the room lit by glow-in-the-dark paint. Hearing and seeing nothing, she continued forward.

At the fountain, she helped herself to some much-needed water and refilled her canteen. Then, faced with a cluster of rails going in all directions, she took out her map. It didn't show the details of any human cities, but it did show the location of several. The headquarters, where her father had told her to go, lay farther south. Salmon City, where Isaac had disappeared, lay to the west.

Wren went west.

Isaac still didn't know whether the voracan was really named Mine, or whether voracans even used names the way humans and clepsits did. It didn't matter. The voracan that Isaac now thought of as Mine had brought another hamburger and soda. It managed to carry the meal without piercing the paper cup, and the root beer quenched Isaac's thirst.

"You speak English," Isaac said when he had finished drinking. He'd had plenty of time to think about this, and it bothered him.

"Yes, yes."

"Why? Don't voracans have their own language?"

"Yes, yes, we talk, not with words, not with words, but with pulses, with electricity. It is not as clear as words, though, so we learned yours. We learned to listen, to spy, to spy." Mine used its quills to shove a wooden box forward. "I found a game for you, a game, a game. So you won't be so bored." Isaac didn't know why Mine cared about his feelings, but he supposed it was because a happy prisoner was less likely to cause trouble. His legs were strapped into the chair at the moment, but his upper body was free. He leaned down to pick up the box.

It was a chessboard. The pieces were inside—most of them anyway. Two pawns were missing, one white and one black.

"Let's play," Mine said. "Let's, let's."

Isaac had played a few times before, but always on a computer, and the program had showed him which moves were possible. On his own, he couldn't remember the rules for each piece. He suspected that Mine knew less, though, so he decided to make up whatever he couldn't recall.

Mine maneuvered the small pieces easily. Although the voracan sometimes used tools that attached to its quills—things that resembled metal thimbles capped with screwdrivers, hammers, or chisels—now it used no such devices. Its many quills jutted in and out in fast, fine movements, forming clusters that pinched the chess pieces.

Isaac stared, mesmerized.

Mine noticed. "The others are clumsy, clumsy. Their minds are dull, dull. This is why I alone can craft the machines."

Isaac thought of the huge storage room filled with various tanks and countless chairs. "You built everything on your own?"

"No, no. I had helpers, scouts to look for treasure, workers to move things. But I designed the plans; I created the firsts. The others just copy, copy. All around the world, they copy my designs, and I fix what they do wrong, fix, fix."

"You designed the chair?" It shouldn't have come as a surprise, but Isaac felt sick at the thought.

"No, no. The chair is special. The design came from above."

Above? Mine must have meant a human. "That's not possible."

"It is. It is. And now I cannot get it to work, and I don't know that I want to. You are not what I thought you would be. Not what I thought."

"So don't do it. Don't fix the chair."

"What choice do I have?" It prodded Isaac's soda cup. "What choice? What choice?"

They finished the game. Isaac won, due in no small part to the advantage gained by inventing the rules as he went. He won the second game, too. He suspected that Mine might have been going easy on him. Which, considering everything, struck him as quite strange.

* * *

Mine returned frequently, sometimes to work on the chair, sometimes to play chess. Isaac never turned down a game. He figured it was smart to keep Mine as busy as possible. Besides, he actually *was* bored.

After a while, the rules—even the fabricated ones— became set. Isaac could no longer make up moves to suit himself. And if Mine had been letting Isaac win before, this wasn't the case anymore.

"You are clever," Mine said, even though it had won the last two rounds. "Not like my kind, not at all, not at all. They have no time for puzzles or games."

"What do voracans do for fun?" Isaac asked. The very idea of a voracan hobby sounded absurd.

"Fight, fight. Hunt, hunt. Things I am no good at."

Mine had seemed plenty good at fighting and hunting when it had skewered Isaac's arms, but maybe voracan standards were different. Isaac set up the board. "Well, you're good at chess."

"Yes, yes, and for this the other voracans hate me."

For a moment Isaac pitied Mine. He knew what it was like not to belong. But the moment of pity didn't last. Mine was his captor. It played chess and delivered hamburgers, but it was still a monster.

"You're building the machines that are supposed to be your victory, aren't you?" Isaac asked. "The other voracans can't hate you." Although humans and clepsits could.

"Yes, yes. Now, now. But for hundreds of years, I built doors, and they stabbed my sensitive flesh. I built lamps, and they snapped my quills. Only when I built weapons did they listen, only then, only then."

Hundreds of years? How long did voracans live?

"Do you think I could go on another walk?" Isaac asked. "I won't try to escape."

"Do you not like the game? Do you not? Do you not?"

"It's great." Although he would have preferred a video game. Or soccer. Or his parents and his house and his freedom. "But it's missing two pieces. If I go to the junk—uh, treasure—room, maybe I can find them."

"But last time, last time—"

"Last time, you caught me easily. Why would I try that again? Please? I need the exercise, and the game will be more fun with the other pieces."

"Yes, yes. Voracans are not good at searching for cold, lifeless objects. This way, this way."

There was only one way to go, but Isaac didn't say anything. He followed Mine out of the small room and down the narrow corridor. He tried to ignore the voracans they passed, all of which managed to look like they were licking their lips despite not having any.

During his first hours underground, voracans seemed to crowd the tunnels. Now, though, Isaac realized that there weren't very many of them, not if this place was supposed to be the voracan version of a city, one that was growing so overcrowded its citizens needed to conquer the world. He wondered where the rest of them were. He hoped never to find out.

When he reached the fork, he didn't even glance toward the passage that led to the machines. Like a good prisoner, he kept close to Mine.

They reached the junk room. Isaac began searching the trash, but he wasn't looking for the missing pawns. He was looking for anything that would help him escape. He didn't know what such an object might be, but he figured he'd recognize it when he saw it.

There was a pile of batteries of every type. The voracans must have used them to power the infrared lamps. There were heaps of car parts, mostly just the seats. The voracans had used the rest already.

There were cell phones. Isaac grabbed one, and his fingers jabbed at its buttons. The screen flashed on. Isaac's heart raced, but he knew he had no real reason to get excited. There was no signal, not so far underground.

"What is it? What? What?"

"Nothing." Isaac was about to throw the useless phone back into the pile, but he changed his mind. He raised it to his ear. "Yes," he said in a loud whisper. "Look for the hole over by the house. Follow that down and you'll find me. I've put trackers everywhere. Bring as big a rescue team as you can gather."

Mine's quills extended as it grasped for the phone, but Isaac dropped it on the ground and smashed it under his foot.

"You joke, joke. Those do not work down here."

Isaac's lips twitched in what was almost an honest-to-goodness smile. He hadn't expected his little trick to work, anyway.

From behind Isaac, quills scratched his leg before piercing the broken remains of the phone. Isaac turned around and found himself face to scary face with another voracan. This one was bigger than Mine, and when it spoke, its voice was shriller.

"Our victory is no joke, our victory, our victory."

It skittered to the wall and opened a previously unseen door, through which it disappeared.

"We must go back to the chair," Mine said. "We must. We must."

Isaac followed, no longer smiling. The other voracan had been right. This was no joke.

This time, Wren changed into the blue pants, pink shirt, and shoes her father had packed. Accustomed to skirts, she had expected the pants to feel stiff and uncomfortable, but these clothes actually allowed her to move more freely than her fur dress ever had. The shoes, with hard soles and long strings that made them much more complicated than the fur slippers she usually wore, were another pleasant surprise. They made it seem as though she were walking on air.

Everything fit perfectly.

Her father had not had time to get human clothing after the letter had arrived. He must have kept a set of human clothes stashed away for her at all times, just in case. He had known the day might come when she would have to flee the clan—a thought that had never even crossed Wren's mind. Not until the arrival of that awful letter, anyway.

The rotten egg odor lingered in her memory. The letter had smelled, just like the voracans that must have sent it. They had stalked her, and they must have stalked Isaac, too. She had escaped them. He hadn't.

She had assumed the voracans had killed him. That was, after all, what the monsters did. According to the stories her siblings and cousins had told her, the voracans drained every last drop of life from their prey. They didn't hold their prey captive.

But the Reads—her parents, she reminded herself—believed that Isaac had been taken, not killed. That was what the arboreal clepsit had said. Maybe the Reads knew something no one else did.

Isaac might be alive somewhere, and everyone was too busy talking about traitors and preparing for war to search for him.

Wren didn't want to prepare for war. She wanted to prevent it. That was the duty of a future ambassador. She also wanted to find her brother. Luckily for her, doing the latter would help her do the former.

And Isaac *was* her brother, even if they shared no blood, even if they had never met. His parents were hers, and her parents were his. That had to make them siblings. More than that, even. Most siblings only shared one set of parents, but they shared two.

Using the clepsit pulley system, she hauled herself and the carriage up to the top of the Salmon City rail station. She decided not to take another nap, although she could have used one, and instead went straight outside.

Peeking out between the clouds, the sun shone down on the town. The building Wren exited was gray and boxy, completely plain except for the rail symbol etched into the door and the numbers painted above it. The other buildings on the path looked far more welcoming, with bright windows and colorful awnings. One had tables and chairs out front, where people sat eating and talking.

The various scents of food lured Wren forward, but before moving even a single step away from the gray building, she made note of the numbers above the door: 546. She also paid careful attention to the green sign that labeled the path. It wasn't a number this time. Instead, the path was called Rose Avenue.

546 Rose Avenue. 546 Rose Avenue. She repeated it over and over to force it into her memory. 546 Rose Avenue.

Wren walked toward the food smells.

Humans used money. She remembered that from Aurora's many lectures on human inferiority. Human society relied on worthless pieces of paper, which they spent all their time collecting, storing, and trading. Sometimes they used credit instead, which was like paper money that didn't actually exist but everyone pretended it did. That didn't make much sense, of course, and Wren felt fairly confident that Aurora had gotten her facts wrong.

But even if the stuff about credit wasn't right, Wren knew that humans used paper. They exchanged the paper for other things. She'd seen the clepsits back in the last city trade their paper for food.

Unfortunately, Wren didn't have any paper of her own. Her father had told her to go straight to the headquarters, so he'd had no reason to supply her with money. Without it, she wouldn't be able to obtain food in a human town. She'd have to settle for the delicious aromas.

Her mouth watered and her stomach rumbled.

She took out some of her fish, much drier than she'd remembered, and nibbled on that while she breathed in the magnificent scents.

A young man approached Wren. A label pinned to his shirt said HI, MY NAME IS DAVID. Humans sure liked putting labels everywhere—even on people.

"Are you looking for someone?" he asked.

"Yes." Wren tried to focus on the task at hand, a difficult proposition when the food smelled so good. "I'm looking for Isaac Read."

"Maybe he's inside," David said.

Wren doubted she'd find her abducted brother inside. He wouldn't be at his burrow, either, but that would still be the best place to start. "Do you know where he lives? It's very important that I find him."

"Uh, sorry. I don't know him."

Of course he didn't. Human towns were big. Really big. It wasn't like living in a clan with several burrows spread out over a few hundred acres of land. Back in the forest, everyone knew everyone. Here, no one knew anyone. "He's a clep—Er, he's a boy about my age. He'll have brown hair and brown eyes this time of year."

"Sorry." David picked up some dirty dishes and went inside with them.

That conversation hadn't gone the way she'd hoped, but at least no one was chasing after her or asking where her parents were. Although she still didn't feel at home among the humans, she fit in much better now that she had the right clothes. It would probably be safe to talk to a few more people.

Wren approached another man. "Do you know where I can find Isaac Read? He's a boy my age, with brown hair."

The man was reading a large sheet of paper and didn't seem happy about the interruption. "Haven't seen him." He raised the sheet of paper to block his face.

Wren walked down the path to another cluster of humans, then another and another. No one knew who Isaac was or where to find him.

"Maybe if you could show us a photograph," a woman suggested before walking away.

Wren didn't have a photograph—she only knew what they were from stories she'd heard—so she continued walking and asking whomever she happened to see. At least her cushioned shoes kept her feet from getting too sore. The shoes really were quite amazing.

She came across a large building. Huge, actually. Hundreds of motored carriages surrounded the two-story structure. The clear doors looked like they consisted of nothing, but they were actually quite heavy and took significant effort to push open.

She expected to find the interior dark and stuffy, like the underground rail stations, but it proved surprisingly bright and airy, with artificial lights everywhere. It smelled good, too, sweet and spicy and delicious. People walked along wide paths, sometimes stopping in one of the many rooms, each of which had hundreds of fine items that could be traded for the right amount of paper.

"Excuse me," Wren asked a woman with two young children passing by. "What is this building?"

"The Salmon City Mall. Are you lost?"

"No. I'm fine." She didn't need more well-intentioned adults trying to haul her off, like the man in the last town had. "I'm looking for Isaac Read, a boy my age, with dark brown hair and eyes, probably a little on the small side." Compared to human kids his age, anyway.

"Sorry, I don't know him. If you go to the information desk, they can probably use the loudspeaker to help you find him."

Wren had never heard of a loudspeaker, but

thanks to the humans' love for labels, she found the information desk easily enough. The man there used a machine—the loudspeaker, Wren guessed—to broadcast her question about Isaac Read to everyone in the mall at once. Then she waited for a while. No one came forward with any information for her.

When she left the mall, the sun was low on the horizon. She'd have to find a place to spend the night soon. First, though, she'd search for Isaac in a few more places.

She was growing tired despite the cushioned shoes she wore. Hungry, too. She ate the rest of her dried fish and all her fruit. If she'd followed her father's instructions, she'd be at the headquarters by now. Running out of food shouldn't have posed a problem.

She came across a field with short, strangely uniform grass. Narrow paths weaved around large, colorful structures that children climbed on. Parents sat on benches and watched.

Wren went from child to child and parent to parent. No one knew of Isaac. As the sky darkened, parents called their children to them, and people began to leave. A few stragglers remained, though, so she continued with her questions.

"Do you know a boy named Isaac Read?" Wren asked two boys and a girl about her age. "He has dark brown hair and eyes."

The girl put down the cards she'd been playing with. "He was supposed to meet us here, but he never showed up. He hasn't answered his phone, either."

"Thanks, anyway." Wren started to walk toward another group of children, although she had little hope left, and her growing exhaustion made it difficult to think, much less walk.

Wait.

Wren stopped. What had the girl said about Isaac? Something about meeting him. That meant she knew him. Finally, someone knew him! "Can you take me to his burrow?"

"Burrow?"

Right. Humans didn't have burrows. They preferred buildings. "Where he lives."

"His house?" asked one of the boys. He wore small pieces of glass in front of his eyes, which struck Wren as very dangerous since glass was prone to breaking. "We went there the other day. There was a—" The girl elbowed him, and he stopped.

"I need to find him. It's very important. He's—"

Wren hesitated, not wanting to give away any secrets. "He's in danger."

"What kind of danger?" the other boy asked. "Does it have anything to do with those green men we saw at his house?"

"You saw arboreal clep—" Wren looked over her shoulder. Clepsits had been in the area recently. Maybe they still were. "Yes. It does. Please, can you take me there?"

The three humans whispered to each other. Wren stood too far away to hear much, but she caught enough to know they were talking about the green men, the arboreal clepsits.

"Sure," the girl said, a question in her voice. "This way."

C oney had arrived at the North American Head-quarters for Clepsit-Human Relations ahead of the others. The rail station connected directly to the headquarters, so as soon as he hauled himself up using the pulley system, he found himself in the basement level of the large building.

He took an elevator—the human kind—up to the main floor. The buttons required some trial and error, and the swooshing doors startled him, but he appreciated the rest his arms received. He never wanted to see another pulley again if he could help it.

The main floor seemed oddly empty and flat, each

smooth surface stretching into another equally smooth surface. There were plants here and there, but they grew in containers and not out of the ground as proper plants should. They might not have even been real.

A human woman sat behind a large table. She smiled. "Can I help you?"

Coney resisted the urge to run. The woman hadn't sounded angry. She didn't know he wasn't supposed to be there. "I'm looking for Wren of Snow."

The woman stared at a box that sat on the table in front of her. "Sorry, she hasn't checked in."

She hadn't checked in? She'd left days before him. How could she not have checked in?

"What's your name?" the woman asked. "Are your parents with you?"

"I'm, uh . . ." Panic formed a knot in Coney's stomach. His parents and—more importantly—his aunt and uncle hadn't arrived yet, but they would soon. When they discovered that he'd sneaked off ahead of them, defying their commands in the process, they would be furious. "I'm Ocean. Of, uh, Night."

The woman frowned at this, even though Coney felt fairly certain that he'd heard of a Night Clan. Luckily, the elevator doors swooshed open again, and out walked a large woman covered in white fur.

"Grace of South," the woman behind the desk said, standing. She signaled two men, both human and both large, who had been sitting nearby, and they came over to help Grace of South with her bags. "I hope you received our message."

"Yes, yes, I received it," she said in a strong accent. She wrinkled her nose at the humans helping her. "I'm very aware of what's happening. That's why I'm here."

Coney tiptoed away. The building, far larger than any burrow he'd ever seen, had to offer plenty of places to hide. He'd wait in the shadows until Wren arrived. And if she didn't come soon, he'd leave the headquarters in search of her.

Wren couldn't shake the feeling that someone was watching her. It was probably just the three humans, whose names she now knew were Sara, Justin, and Ryan. They kept sneaking peeks at her when they thought she wasn't looking, and for good reason. She clearly didn't fit into human society. For one thing, she kept thinking of it as "human" society. Other humans, knowing nothing of clepsits, probably just thought of it as society.

She pushed and pulled on the door to the Reads' house, but it didn't budge. "How do you get into human houses?" she asked, cringing as the word "human" slipped out. She had to stop doing that.

"Uh, you could try ringing the doorbell," Sara said.

"Or knocking," Justin added.

"Or breaking a window," Ryan suggested, pointing to one of the glass sections of the wall. Humans seemed really fond of these windows, though Wren couldn't understand why. What was the point of having a wall you could see through? Didn't that defeat the purpose of a wall?

Sara elbowed Ryan in the stomach. "Don't listen to him. About anything. Ever."

Wren pressed a button next to the door to ring the doorbell, but nothing happened. She assumed the sound must have been meant to alert whoever was inside to her presence, but of course no one was inside. Isaac was either dead or missing, and his parents had gone to the headquarters, where she was supposed to be.

Sara pushed Justin away while fanning her hand in front of her nose. "Eww, Justin, what did you eat for lunch? Old eggs?"

"Hey, it wasn't me," Justin said.

"Me neither," Ryan added. "She who smelt it dealt it."

Wren smelled it, too. Rotten eggs. The stench of sulfur. The stink of voracans. The sun had almost finished setting; only a few rays of pink remained on the horizon. The shadows had grown long, providing ample places for the voracans to hide.

"Hey, what's this?" Justin picked up a long black quill he'd found on the ground. He held it like a sword.

Wren took the voracan quill from him. It gave off a slight odor, but not enough to explain the strong rotten egg stench they'd noticed.

Wren was more convinced than ever. The Reads had been telling the truth when they blamed the voracans for Isaac's disappearance. The voracans had taken Isaac. They lingered in the area, though for what purpose Wren didn't know.

"I need to get inside," she said. "Now." The house looked warm and safe. If it was anything like the other human structures she'd encountered, there would be some artificial light inside, perhaps enough to keep the voracans at bay.

"We could try the back door and the windows," Ryan suggested. "Maybe they left something open."

Sara rolled her eyes. "And again, I remind you not to listen to him. We can't just sneak into other people's houses." She lowered her voice, addressing only her two friends. "We don't even know who she is."

"But she knows about the green men," Justin whispered back. "Don't you want to find out more?"

"I'm their daughter," Wren said, eager to interrupt the conversation about arboreal clepsits. "I'm Isaac's sister." Another whiff of sulfur wafted on the breeze. "We need to hurry."

The three humans exchanged a look.

"If you're Isaac's sister," Sara asked, "why didn't you know where he lived?"

"It's complicated." She hesitated. She couldn't tell them everything, but she had to tell them something or they wouldn't help. "I was raised by another family. The Reads are my parents, though. Isaac's in danger. We are, too, so we need to get inside."

"Why are we in danger?" Justin asked. "Is it because of the green men?"

The sulfuric odor intensified. It made Wren's eyes water and caused her to gag.

"Capture them, capture, capture."

A snarl of black quills sprang forward. Wren thrust the quill Justin had found into the center of the creature. The voracan stopped, the quill grinding and cracking within it.

Three more voracans burst from a hole in the ground.

Wren no longer needed to urge her human companions to hurry. They ran left, then swerved right as two more voracans joined the chase, and ended up trapped by the side of the Reads' house. Sara grabbed a loose stone—part of a small footpath—and chucked it at a window, which shattered into sharp shards of glass.

The four humans climbed inside.

Justin flipped a switch, and light poured out of a fixture on the ceiling.

They knew about the voracan weakness, Wren thought. But no, that didn't make sense. They hadn't been able to identify the black quill. Or the green men. Justin had turned on the light because he was a human, born and—unlike Wren—raised. Humans always shunned the darkness. Even Wren, with her limited understanding of human culture, had gleaned that much. That was why they put artificial lights everywhere.

In any case, Justin's instincts saved them, for the moment anyway. The voracans retreated—but not quietly. As they slinked into the outside darkness, one of them said, "Your rescue mission has failed, failed. We have found you."

Sara, Justin, and Ryan turned to Wren, and although she had much to learn about human society, she felt quite certain of one more thing. They wanted an explanation.

The voracans searched every inch of the room where they kept Isaac, every crevice in the dirt walls, and every fissure in the ground, but they turned up nothing. They searched Isaac's chair, too—several times in fact—and Isaac himself. Their quills stabbed him carelessly during these inspections, but he enjoyed watching them panic.

Unfortunately, their surveillance of him had increased. Mine still came to work on the chair, but there was no more time for games of chess.

The voracans usually entered the way they always

had: through the doorless opening that led to the corridor. Other times, though, they used a previously hidden passageway.

The lair was larger and more complicated than Isaac had realized. That explained why he saw so few voracans for what was supposed to be a growing population. The rest of them stayed in corridors and rooms closed to Isaac, hidden behind shut doors he hadn't even noticed.

One of these corridors had to lead to the surface. To freedom.

The infrared lamps were important. They acted as markers, not lights. Isaac should have figured that out sooner. The voracans didn't care for light, but the heat showed them where the doors were.

While Mine worked on the chair, Isaac leaned against the wall next to one of the lamps. He had to look casual—Mine wasn't the only voracan around—but he was trying to examine the door. There were no handles or knobs. How did it open?

"Get away from there, away, away." A voracan prodded him back toward the chair—which meant that he was getting close to something.

Close wasn't good enough. He needed to escape. He needed a new tactic.

Before, he'd upset the voracans by pretending to talk to someone. Maybe a little more upheaval would do the trick. He didn't have the cell phone anymore, but that didn't matter. It hadn't worked, anyway.

When he knew that some of the voracans were watching, he spoke into his wrist as if he were wearing some sort of device. "I've convinced a few voracans to join our side. All really big guys," he added so they wouldn't suspect Mine. "They'll help you get in. Gotta go. I'll be in touch soon."

He pretended to throw the imaginary device into the corridor.

Shouting erupted among the voracans.

"It's there, there."

"You're stepping on it, stepping, stepping."

"Traitor, traitor."

The shouts faded when the fighting began. Isaac had hoped for as much. Voracans always seemed to be looking for a reason to fight.

The brawling voracans became a tangled mass. Some used their quills to jab at each other's soft centers, while others tried to catch the spikes and break them. They hissed and howled as quills snapped off and clattered to the ground.

They had asked for a war, and they'd gotten it.

Isaac resumed his examination of the door. Mine, who had stayed out of the fights, didn't try to stop him.

Another voracan approached—the biggest Isaac had seen yet, with quills as thick as his wrists yet still as sharp as razors. It swatted Isaac away from the door.

Isaac swallowed his fear and forced a smile. "Thanks for helping me," he said, loudly enough for the other voracans to hear. They'd stopped fighting and were watching now. "You'll take care of the others, right?"

"Your plan won't work. We have found your so-called rescue team, so-called, so-called."

They had found it? Isaac had made up the rescue team, but if the voracans had found one, one had to exist. Which meant someone was coming to save him.

"So what if you have?" Isaac said, trying to keep the surprise and the hope out of his voice. "There are reinforcements on the way."

"A handful of mere children, mere children. They pose no threat to us." The large voracan forced Isaac back into the chair. Its clumsy quills couldn't work the restraints, but it prodded Mine to do the work. "We shall capture them and bring them here, more subjects for our machines, more marrow for us to eat, more food to make us strong, more, more."

30

"What were those spiky things?" Justin demanded.

"Are they related to the green men we saw earlier?" Ryan asked.

"No! Clepsits and voracans aren't related. They—" Wren bit her lip. She wasn't allowed to reveal clepsit secrets, but in a way, she wouldn't be revealing anything. These human children had already seen clepsits and voracans. She would merely be providing a little clarification. Besides, the humans obviously weren't going to drop the issue, and Wren needed someone to trust, someone who could help her.

She told them about everything: the clepsits, the voracans, her missing brother, and the looming war.

"But don't tell anyone," she added quickly.

"Who would believe us?" Ryan asked, a dazed look in his glass-covered eyes. "I'm not even sure I believe it, and I saw those spiky voracan things with my own eyes."

"I believe it," Justin said. "I've always suspected there were elves and dragons and stuff out there."

Elves and dragons? Wren had no idea what those were, but she decided not to ask. She needed to keep the conversation focused. "How am I supposed to find Isaac now that the voracans are chasing me again? I don't even know where to look."

Sara stared at the broken window, but she didn't go near it. Like the others, she stayed in the center of the living room, directly underneath the artificial light that hung from the ceiling. "You need to find the voracans' lair, and the voracans want to take you there." She paused. "Why don't you let them?"

Wren's mouth fell open.

Why? Because they were the stuff of nightmares. Because the thought of being near them was enough to send shivers down her spine, and the prospect of being carried away by them sent her into full panic.

Because they might kill her. "Because I'm not an idiot. If the voracans capture me, they win."

"Not necessarily," Sara said. "The voracans have to have a weakness. You just need to find what it is and use it against them. What do you know about them?"

"Not much." Wren recalled the stories her siblings and cousins used to tell her, back when she could still convince herself it was all made up. "They live underground. They drink marrow."

"What's marrow?" Ryan asked.

"The stuff inside bones," Justin explained. "It's where blood cells are made."

Sara nodded. "Okay, okay, the creepy things want to suck our marrow. What else?"

"They don't like light," Justin said. He looked up at the artificial light above them and winced. "Speaking of which, shouldn't we be looking for flashlights or something? Those monster spikes could cut power lines easy, and if the lights go out, we're toast."

"And speaking of toast," Ryan said, "did the Reads leave any food here? It's way past dinnertime."

"Yeah, my mom's probably wondering where I am. Which is totally her fault for not getting me a cell phone," Sara added.

The Reads had plenty of food. After taking stock

of the options, Sara announced that they should have turkey and cheese sandwiches.

"Fine," Ryan said, "but I'm having mine without bread. That stuff will kill me."

Wren examined the soft brown rectangle that, according to its plastic wrapping, was bread. "How can it kill you?"

"It can't," Justin promised, and he stuffed a piece into his mouth as evidence.

Wren was more suspicious of the orange squares, which didn't look or feel like anything she had ever eaten before. She took a cautious bite. Then a less cautious bite. Then she shoved what was left into her mouth. "This is good. What is it made from?"

"Milk," Sara asked. "Old milk. It's best not to think about it. Haven't you ever had cheese before?"

"No. Clepsits gather fruits, vegetables, and nuts, and they hunt animals. They don't eat milk." Or old milk. Wren frowned. It hadn't tasted old.

"You mean adults don't," Ryan said. "Babies must, right?"

"No. Hatchlings don't drink milk."

Justin's jaw dropped. "Hatchlings? You mean clepsits hatch? Like from eggs?"

"Yes." Wren grabbed another piece of cheese. "I'm famished."

After dinner, they searched the house for flashlights. Well, Sara, Ryan, and Justin did. Wren tried to help, but she didn't know what a flashlight was or what one might look like, which made the search more difficult. She tried to appear confident, though. These people wouldn't help her if they thought she was weak.

"Found one," Justin said, picking up a blue cylinder that had been lying on the floor. He pushed a button, and out streamed a beam of light.

"This must be Isaac's bedroom," Ryan said. "He doesn't have any brothers or sisters, right?"

"He has lots of siblings, but yeah, none who live here." Wren stared at the bed, a soft rectangle covered with blankets of varying thickness, which Isaac had had all to himself. If he and Wren hadn't switched places, the bed would have been hers. She never would have suffered sleepless nights plagued by snores and kicks.

"Here's his cell phone," Sara said, pointing to a sleek black device that sat on a table by his bed.

"There's no password." After pressing a few

buttons, Ryan used the phone to talk to his parents. He told them he was spending the night at Justin's. Then Justin used the phone to tell his parents he was sleeping over at Ryan's. Finally, Sara called her parents to say that she was staying over at Rebecca's house. Wren had no idea who Rebecca was.

"They wouldn't believe us if we told them the truth, and we can't go home while those monsters are probably still watching us," Justin told Wren, even though Wren hadn't commented on the lies. She'd been too fascinated by the way the phone worked. It certainly beat having pigeons deliver messages.

The four of them sat on Isaac's bed, which was even more comfortable than it looked.

"Are all human burrows—houses—like this? How many people usually live in them?" Wren knew that Isaac and his parents—her parents—lived alone, but that was because Isaac had to keep his identity a secret.

Sara shrugged. "Some houses are smaller. Some are bigger. Most families have about four to five people, but some are really big, like seven or eight people."

That didn't sound big to Wren.

"Are the burrows underground?" Justin asked. "I

mean, they must be, or they're not burrows, but that's really weird."

"What's weird about it? Clepsit homes are safe and well insulated. They don't require chopping down an entire forest just to get the wood to build walls." That was what Aurora said. But why was Wren quoting Aurora? Why was she praising clepsit burrows, which were also cramped and dark? Something about Justin's tone made her angry.

Was that how all ambassadors felt? Torn between despising and defending their homes? Always an outsider, unable to fit into human or clepsit society?

"Uh, back to the monsters," Sara said, looking uncomfortable. "They drink marrow. They don't like light. Do they have any other weaknesses?"

Once again, Wren thought back to the horror stories she'd grown up with. Most of them involved a child (in the stories her siblings and cousins told, the child always looked like Wren) who got lost. Alone, the child would wander into a dark patch of forest, or possibly fall into a hole. The child might try to hide quietly, but the voracan would sense the child anyway. It would attack, leaving behind a lifeless body.

In one variation, the doomed child, who looked

like Wren, escaped the voracan by fleeing into a thunderstorm. It worked until lightning struck the child—a fate only slightly better than being drained by a voracan.

"They can't see or hear very well," Wren said. "And they can't smell at all. They track their prey another way. Thunderstorms disorient them."

"It sounds like they have some sort of electro-reception," Justin said. "Hammerhead sharks have it, and some other animals, too. They sense the electric fields that living organisms produce and use that to locate their prey. It's unusual in land animals, but not unheard of."

Ryan stared at his friend. "How do you know that?"

"How *don't* you? It's in our biology textbook. We had a test on it last semester."

Sara laughed. "The only thing Ryan learns in biology is the exact shade of Valerie's hair. He sits behind her in every class and practically drools over her back."

Ryan nodded. "It's light brown with strawberry-blond highlights. Could we use the electro-whatever to help Wren?"

Justin nodded his head slowly. "Yeah, I think we

can come up with some sort of device. Yeah. I'll need some of the supplies back at my house, but I can do it."

"There you go, Wren." Sara patted her on the back. "Tomorrow afternoon, you'll have something to help you. Tomorrow night, you can let the voracans take you. By Monday, you'll have found Isaac."

Wren forced herself to smile. "Great."

Isaac was no longer allowed out of the chair. Mine continued to tinker with the marrow-draining system, which still didn't work, while Isaac sat there, an unwilling test-subject-in-waiting. A large voracan watched over both of them, jabbing Isaac with sharp quills if he dared to move.

The infrared lamps marked the doors. If Isaac could just get a little time to himself, away from the chair, he could figure out how to open the doors.

He needed to do it quickly. If his escape was to be successful, it had to happen before Mine fixed the machine. Once the horrible contraption started draining

Isaac's marrow again, he'd be in too much pain to do anything useful. He cringed at the memory of his first day in the voracans' lair, when his body ached from his brief time hooked up to the malfunctioning chair.

But he didn't attempt to flee. Instead, he slept. The long hours spent prodded by angry voracans had made him tired. There wasn't anything else to do, anyway—not while he was stuck in the chair and monitored.

At least he could dream of escape, of his home and his parents. He dreamed that his dad was making cookies for him: gooey chocolate chip cookies, as many as he wanted.

A whirring sound woke him.

The chair. The chair was making noise.

"Does it work?" the large voracan asked. "Does it? Does it?"

Using a pair of pliers that were fixed to one of its quills, Mine yanked a tube loose. The whirring stopped. "Not yet, no, no."

The larger voracan prodded Mine with a quill. "Soon, we will have others to fill the chairs. Others to supply us with marrow. You must get it working. You must. You must."

Mine was silent until the other voracan shambled

toward the exit. Then Mine spoke to Isaac. "I miss our games. The others cannot play, not like you, not like you."

Mine resumed its work on the chair.

Supposedly.

A theory was forming in Isaac's groggy mind.

The machine had whirred. It had worked—until Mine had stopped it. Mine had admitted to disliking the chairs. Perhaps it was slowing its progress intentionally.

But the work could not be slowed forever. Isaac drifted back to his dream world, where his parents awaited him.

As soon as the sun's rays spilled over the horizon, Sara, Justin, and Ryan left. They promised to return before sunset, but until then, Wren had the entire house to herself.

Sara had showed her how the bathroom worked. Water poured from faucets, each of which had a different purpose. This struck Wren as absurd. Why should this water be for drinking and that water be for bathing? Wasn't it all the same? She didn't want to disrespect human customs, though, so she did everything exactly as instructed. It wasn't all bad. The standing bath—a shower, Sara had called it, and it was quite similar to rain showers only much, much warmer—soothed her sore muscles and washed away her worries, if only for a moment. She took two.

She cleaned up the broken glass from when they'd forced their way into the house, but she didn't have a clue about how to go about repairing the window. Humans must keep extra glass around, she reasoned, considering how easily the material broke and how often it must need replacing, but she couldn't find any anywhere.

Her search of the house revealed no further clues about the voracans, either, but Wren did find something from clepsit culture. Isaac had a statue of two clepsits with their tails linked in a symbol of good luck. Wren compared it to her own and found the two almost identical. Her father—his father—must have carved both of them.

Mrs. Read had never sent a gift to Wren. Not even once. Not even a tiny bauble or a morsel of human chocolate, which she'd eaten for the first time last night. Apparently, humans had tons of the delicious stuff—Isaac even kept a few candy bars in his bedroom—but Mrs. Read had never thought to give any to Wren.

Which was for the best. Her cousins and siblings

would have destroyed anything from the human world. Mrs. Read must have known that. Otherwise, she would have sent something.

All the same, it would have been nice of her to try.

A piece of paper sat next to the clepsit statue on the shelf. Wren unfolded it and read the note scribbled inside. It was a message to Isaac from his parents, telling him to find them at the North American Headquarters. Wren slipped the note into her pocket. She'd give it to Isaac herself.

In another bedroom, one that appeared to belong to Mr. and Mrs. Read, Wren found a book of pictures. Each one depicted the Reads in glossy, colorful detail. Iron had said that humans used photography to capture images—it was one of the few things Aurora couldn't find a way to criticize—but Wren had never seen it before this trip. The images seemed real enough to move, but no matter how long she stared, everything in the photograph stayed still, as if frozen in time.

Throughout her search, she kept every light in the house on, and she carried the flashlight with her just in case.

Once, when she was near the broken window, she thought she caught a whiff of rotten eggs. The voracans preferred the dark, but they would attack in daylight, too, as long as they could stay in the shadows. She didn't see or hear any sign of the creatures, though, so maybe she'd imagined the stench.

When the sun dragged itself up to its midday peak, Sara, Justin, and Ryan had not yet returned. And as the sun slowly made its way back to the horizon, Wren remained alone. The shadows stretched, and darkness loomed.

They might not come back. They had promised to, but how much could the promise of a stranger mean? They weren't part of Wren's clan.

Wren concluded that after careful consideration, they had—quite wisely—decided to stay away. She would have to come up with another plan to find Isaac. Or, if she couldn't think of anything, she could go to the headquarters. That was what her father had wanted her to do. Maybe he had been right.

Besides, even if Justin and the others returned with the device they'd promised, what chances did Wren have against the entire voracan population? Venturing into their underground lair with some toy made by a human boy she barely knew did not strike her as a well-planned strategy—more like a lost cause. Of course she couldn't go ahead with this crazy idea, even if they did come back, which they clearly wouldn't.

A bell rang. Wren couldn't pinpoint the origin of the tone, but she recognized the sound from the other day. Someone was at the door.

She considered ignoring the sound. What if voracans had learned to operate the doorbell? It could be a trap. She had to be smart about such matters.

The bell rang again. "Come on, Wren! It's us," yelled a voice that sounded very much like Sara's, and not at all like that of a voracan. "It's going to get dark soon."

Wren opened the door. Sara, Justin, and Ryan hurried inside, shutting and locking the door behind them. Some of the sun's rays seeped in through the windows, but they gathered under the light in the living room anyway.

They probably didn't have the device. Humans were good with technology, true, but Justin hadn't even reached adulthood yet. And he'd only had one afternoon. Of course he couldn't actually deliver the device as promised. They'd have to abandon the plan, which had been reckless anyway.

Wren wasn't being cowardly, merely realistic.

Justin handed her a sleek metal rectangle with several buttons and a long, cylindrical piece that jutted out of it. "This should mess with the voracans' senses," he whispered, shooting glances at the broken window.

"He's been calling it an electro-no-ception device," Ryan said, "because he's a dork."

"I've been calling it an electro-no-ception device because it stops the voracans' electroreception, so there's no electroreception. In theory. And I have to call it something." Justin looked at the window again. "But not too loudly. They might be listening. You'll have to keep pressing these buttons until you find the right setting, and then keep it there. Leave it off when you're not using it so it doesn't run out of power. Don't let anyone see it, and if anyone finds it, don't tell them I made it. They might think it's a cell phone jammer, and those things are, uh, kind of illegal."

Sara laughed. "You really are a dork! She's going into an underground monster city where she's considered food to rescue a boy who may not even be alive so she can stop a war that could destroy the planet, and you're worried about getting caught with a cell phone jammer?"

Wren laughed, too, just to be polite. Humans had a strange sense of humor.

"The war you're trying to prevent," Ryan said,

"might have started already. There's a city in Wyoming—Pacis—that's under some sort of siege. It's been all over the news."

Sara nodded. "Yeah. The government says it's a group of ecoterrorists, but some of the videos and pictures show people with fur. Not fur coats, but actual fur, like an animal. And there are people with green skin, like the men we saw, and people with tails."

"They're different types of clepsits," Wren explained, horrified. "Humans are seeing them? They know about clepsits now?"

"No," Sara said. "Everyone thinks it's just makeup and costumes and stuff, a publicity stunt to gain attention for the protest."

"A couple of tabloids and Internet nuts have said it could be real," Ryan added. "Mutations from nuclear waste, genetic modification, chemtrails, something like that. But nobody listens to them."

Wren hardly understood any of that. What were tabloids and chemtrails? What type of a tree was an Internet, and how could its nuts say anything?

She decided to focus on something she *did* understand.

"Pacis, Wyoming, is where the headquarters are," she said. It was where the Reads were, too. It was where Wren was supposed to be. Maybe it was good she hadn't gone after all.

"There have been other sightings, too," Sara added. "People all over the world have reported being attacked by spiny creatures. No one believes them, of course. All the cases have happened in the middle of nowhere, and there have been a couple of pictures, but they're so blurry that no one can tell what they're looking at. We know, though."

"The voracans have been coming up to the surface to feed." Wren looked at the device and took a deep breath. "So now I wait for the voracans to take me? And then when I find Isaac, I use this device to scramble their senses so we can escape, right?"

Justin smiled weakly. "That's the gist of it."

"What will you do?"

Justin exchanged a look with Sara and Ryan. "Well, uh, we, uh, we need to get back home. See, we have school tomorrow, so we can't tell our parents we're sleeping over at a friend's house again. It's getting dark, so we should actually be heading back now. Will you be all right?"

"Yeah. Yes. Of course." Wren slipped the device into one of her pants pockets, though the cylindrical piece was too long to fit and stuck out awkwardly. Her other pocket bulged with Isaac's phone, the map her father had given her, and the key to the rail stations. "It'll be easy. I'm fine."

"You know," Ryan said. "If you want to wait until tomorrow, that would be okay. We'd understand. Or maybe you could wait until the weekend, when we'd be able to help more."

Wren held her head high. "No. Why would I want to wait? You said it yourself. The war's already started. I can't waste any more time. You guys should go. Thanks for your help, but you're right. It's going to get dark soon."

There was an awkward moment, but then the three of them started toward the door. "Call us when you get back," Sara said. "Our numbers are in Isaac's phone. Good luck."

"Good luck," Ryan and Justin echoed.

They scanned the front yard, gave the air a couple of good sniffs, and hurried down the concrete path.

Alone again, Wren made herself a sandwich, only to find she was too nervous to eat it. Outside, the setting sun splashed the sky with pinks and oranges. Soon, the voracans wouldn't have to stick to the bushes and the shadows. They could roam as they pleased. They could take what they wanted.

Wren turned off the lights.

For a while, nothing happened. She forced herself to take a bite of the sandwich—she couldn't rescue Isaac on an empty stomach—and ended up devouring it in mere seconds. She got up to make another, but a horrible odor caused her to lose her newfound appetite.

The voracans had arrived. One, two, three— Wren tried to count them as they grabbed her, but their spiky bodies blended together. She didn't need an exact number to know that there were too many to fight. Anyway, she wasn't supposed to fight them, not yet.

"Where is the rest of the rescue team? Where? Where?"

She didn't answer. She didn't know how to answer. She had no rescue team—never had. She was, as always, alone.

The voracans' quills dug into her skin. After that, everything was painful and blurred and fast, but she registered being dragged outside. Then cold moist dirt replaced the air. She was underground, a captive in the voracans' territory, far past the point of no return.

33

There was an enormous room devoted to food, and it was food unlike anything Coney had ever tasted before: sweet cakes layered with rich creams, meats seasoned with herbs and spices, thin slices of potatoes that crunched in the most satisfying way. There was so much that no one noticed when he took a little here, a little there.

Coney felt bad about sneaking around, but he assured himself that he wasn't actually doing anything wrong. The food was meant for clepsits and humans. He was a clepsit. That he chose to eat while crouching under tables instead of sitting in the cafeteria made little difference. Nevertheless, not wanting to risk trouble, he was careful not to get caught.

Because the cooks gossiped as they worked, the kitchen was a source not only of food, but also of information. Coney learned that the rest of his family had arrived soon after him, as expected. He still hadn't learned of Wren's whereabouts, though, so he returned to the kitchen regularly for whatever news had come in—and, while he was there, a snack.

At the moment, Coney was sitting under a cart eating a piece of chicken that had, through a stroke of genius, been dipped in flour and submerged in hot oil, making it both juicy and crispy at once. Two clepsit cooks, oblivious to him, chatted away.

"Franny quit," said the small green clepsit woman.

"Can't say I blame her," replied the other clepsit woman, this one blue with webbed fingers. "Larry and Darrin, those two security guards, quit, too. At least that's what I've been told. I think they might have been forced to leave. The place is getting bad for humans."

"Yeah. I've heard the Reads are practically being held prisoner in their room."

So the Reads were here. Maybe they knew where Wren was.

***

By the time Coney found the Reads' room, they had already been moved. According to another bit of kitchen gossip, they were now in the basement. At first, Coney thought this meant they were leaving— the rail station was in the basement—but as the conversation went on, he realized that the basement was divided into two parts. One half contained the rail station. The other half contained the prison.

The Reads were in the latter half.

Sneaking into the prison was harder than sneaking into the kitchen. There were guards everywhere, all of whom were—Coney noted—clepsit. He hadn't seen a single human in over a day.

Right now, two clepsit men watched the entrance. Both came from Antarctica, with the same large body and white fur as Grace of South. They did not talk to each other, choosing instead to stare at the door they guarded in silence.

Coney watched from the shadows. He wasn't sure how much time passed, but it was more than enough for his worries to take hold of him. Helping himself to food was one thing. Breaking into a prison was quite another. It was wrong.

But if Wren was right and the Reads were innocent, then keeping them locked up was wrong, too. What was a person supposed to do when no options were right?

What he had to.

Coney had to help Wren.

A clepsit—one who looked like Coney and the members of his clan, but whom Coney didn't recognize—entered. After a whispered conversation with the two guards, he and one of the guards left. A few minutes later, yelling rang out from the floor above, and the remaining guard hurried away to assist.

Coney seized the opportunity to enter the prison.

There were several cells, many occupied—and all by humans. The place stank of rot and sweat, and flies buzzed around a trash can. One cell contained two humans who looked vaguely familiar: a woman with Wren's red hair and a man with Wren's angular face.

"Are you the Reads?" Coney asked.

"Yes," the woman, Mrs. Read, said. For a woman in a dirty prison cell, she smiled brightly.

The man with her, Mr. Read, also smiled. "You look just like Isaac."

So that was why they were happy to see him. He reminded them of their missing son. And if they were glad to be reminded of him, they must have loved him. They couldn't have hurt him. Wren had been right; her parents were innocent. "I'm Isaac's brother. Wren's brother. Do you know where she is?"

Their smiles faded. "No," Mrs. Read said. "She's missing? For how long?"

Footsteps approached. Coney jumped into the trash can. He couldn't see much from inside the smelly hiding spot, but he caught a few dim peeks through a crack in the container.

The two guards and the messenger entered, along with three other clepsits. The first two had their hands and tails tied behind their backs. The guards pushed them into an empty cell. The other clepsit, a woman, trailed behind everyone else. She appeared to be overseeing the event.

Despite not being able to see very well, Coney recognized all of them instantly. The first two—the prisoners—were his parents, Bronco and Breeze of Snow. The third clepsit was his aunt, Aurora of Snow.

In Isaac's dreams, he escaped the voracans again and again, each time returning to the beautiful and sunny surface world, where his parents greeted him with beaming smiles. Each time, he awoke in the same dank room.

He couldn't do anything to change his situation. He'd never been able to, not once in his entire life. Everything was decided for him by others. When those others had been his parents, it hadn't been so bad, but now monsters controlled him.

Mine was tinkering with the chair.

"Why do you always work on this one?" Isaac asked. "It's not like you don't have any others."

"This way, I can test it fast, fast." In a slightly quieter voice, it added, "And you are clever, clever. We can play, play. We can talk, talk."

But they didn't talk then. They didn't play. There were too many other voracans around. With nothing else to do, Isaac drifted back to sleep.

* * *

Voices infiltrated Isaac's dreams.

"Where is the rescue team? Where? Where?"

"There is only she, only she. The others fled. But she has been identified, yes, yes. She is the human, the ambassador's daughter, the one we sought before."

"We do not need her anymore. The war has already begun. It has. It has."

"We still need her marrow, delicious, delicious. We have brought you another chair. Put her in it. Make the chairs work. Make them. Make them."

A blur of whimpers and yelps followed. Still more or less asleep, Isaac was only vaguely aware of them.

Silence fell. Isaac's dreams returned to visions of

his escape, his parents, the sun. Everything was warm and happy as he drifted deeper into sleep.

"Isaac!" his mother whispered, but her voice sounded strange. Too fearful. Too young. "Isaac, is that you?"

Isaac's eyes opened reluctantly.

A girl—a human girl—was strapped into a chair placed next to his. "You're Isaac, aren't you? You look just like Coney."

Isaac tried to rub his eyes, but the metal constraints around his arms made this impossible. A few blinks would have to suffice in clearing his sleep-blurred vision. "Who are you?"

"Wren. I'm your parents' daughter. The Reads' daughter. The one you switched places with."

Isaac didn't need the explanation. He recognized her name. And now, feeling more awake and really looking at her, he recognized some of her features, too. His mother's hair. His father's face shape. He missed them so much that looking at her almost hurt. "Is Coney my brother?" His parents didn't talk much about his siblings, but he'd heard their names occasionally.

"One of them. The Reads had nothing to do with this, right? Everyone thinks they killed you, but that can't be true, because here you are. The voracans did this, and they framed your parents, didn't they?"

"Of course my parents didn't do this. The voracans are trying to start a war. The clepsits really believe my parents were a part of this? Bronco believes that?"

"Not Bronco. But everyone else. Almost everyone else. That's why I'm here to rescue you." She squirmed in her chair. "How do we get out of here?"

Isaac hesitated. He had so many questions for Wren: What was the clan like? What was Bronco like? How many brothers and sisters did he have? He imagined that the ambassador program must have been fun for her, since she didn't have to worry about hiding her identity.

He had other questions, too, darker ones about why the clepsits had turned on the Reads so easily, and what they intended to do about it now.

It should have been a great family reunion, but there was nothing great about it. They were stuck in the enemies' lair. Wren was here to rescue him, but she didn't even know how to get out of her chair.

He had to stay hopeful.

Maybe she was just one member of the mission. More were coming.

With all the questions competing for attention

in his mind, he settled on the one that mattered the most. "Are you part of the rescue team?"

"Why does everyone keep asking me that? There's no team. Just me." She squirmed again but couldn't wriggle free. "What is this machine?"

Isaac explained how the chair was supposed to work and what the voracans planned to do with them.

Tears streamed down Wren's cheek, but her expression remained stoic and she didn't make any sniffling sounds. It was almost like she was trying to hide her crying, although Isaac couldn't understand why she would bother. Who wouldn't cry in such a situation?

"This is a stupid plan," she said. "I knew it was a stupid plan, but I went ahead with it anyway, and now look at me. Even if the electro-no-ception device works and I scramble the voracans' electroreception, I'll never find my way out of here."

Isaac's eyes widened. For a second, he wondered whether he was still dreaming. His bored brain might have produced Wren as an exciting new twist in the normal escape sequence. It didn't seem like one of his dreams, though. For one thing, he was still stuck in the machine, and he usually freed himself from it as soon as his fantasies began.

Mine stood several yards away, where it talked to one of the larger voracan guards. Isaac didn't think the voracans could hear them, but he spoke in a whisper just in case. "You have a device that can scramble the voracans' senses?"

"Yes." Wren tried rather clumsily to wipe her tears away with her shoulder. "What does it matter, though? We'd still be trapped down here. I can't use it, anyway. I can't even move my hands."

"Don't worry about that," Isaac whispered. "We'll find a way."

Wren squinted, then forced her eyes wide open, then squinted again. It did no good. She could see Isaac, who sat near her, almost close enough to touch. Beyond that, she could make out only vague, shadowy shapes—nothing in detail. Electric lights dotted the underground tunnels, but they were far dimmer than the ones used by humans. Red, too. Isaac seemed to manage fairly well in the almost-complete darkness, but Wren's human eyes refused to adjust.

How was she supposed to carry out a rescue mission when she couldn't even see? Or do *anything* when she couldn't move from her strange mechanical chair? Isaac had told her what it was for. She shuddered, not wanting to think about it.

Despite being almost blind, she sensed a voracan's approach: its rotten egg stench and the soft click-clack of its quills. Her shoulders tensed. She wanted to run away, but metal clamps kept her in place.

Next to her, Isaac remained calm. "It's just Mine," he said. "I don't know if that's its real name, but it's okay."

"It's okay"? Wren didn't understand how anything about the current situation could be *okay*. Maybe the word was defined differently in human society.

The voracan's quills whizzed around her arms, and the metal restraints on her arms clicked open. She still couldn't reach the device in her pocket—the clamps around her hips and legs prevented it—but her hands were free, and that was something.

Was this what Isaac meant when he said this voracan was okay?

The voracan handed her a paper bag and cup. The cup contained an overly sweet beverage that bubbled strangely on her tongue. The bag contained a sandwich, but it was a round piece of meat stuffed between two round pieces of bread—a little different from the ones she'd had earlier. She ate it, and she might have actually liked it if her stomach weren't so knotted.

"Can you let us out of our chairs?" Isaac asked. "Please. We need to stretch."

Mine, the supposedly okay voracan, looked at the other voracans standing guard near the exit. "Now that the rescue team has been caught, they are not watching so closely. But they are still watching. They are. They are. I cannot help you anymore. I must fix the machine, for real, no more games. I am sorry. I am sorry."

Please? Sorry? This was not the type of exchange Wren had expected to hear. It wasn't the kind she cared to participate in, either.

She screamed.

"What is wrong?" Mine asked. "What? What?"

She kept screaming.

The voracan drew closer to investigate.

She didn't have any sticks this time, so her hand would have to do. She reached for the voracan's soft center, pinching and prodding and doing anything she could to hurt the monster. As its spikes stabbed her arms, her fake screams morphed into real ones.

With her other hand, she grabbed one of the quills, long and thin, and yanked. It snapped off.

"What is going on? What? What?" This came from a different voracan, one with a shriller voice.

"Nothing. Nothing," Mine said. "The chair is almost done. Almost. Almost. I have discovered the design flaw. Now I must make new tools to fix it, new tools, new tools."

Mine left. A moment later, the other voracan skittered away, too, though its stench remained strong, suggesting it had not gone far.

"Are you trying to make them angry?" Isaac whispered.

"Why shouldn't I?" Wren answered. "Are you trying to make friends with them?"

She'd had to do something. She'd keep trying things, too, until she succeeded or until she lost—anything was better than admitting defeat.

* * *

The lamps that lit the burrow often ran out of oil during the night, so Wren was accustomed to waking up in a dark room. This was different, though. The chair.

The clamps. The monsters. Compared to the voracans, Opal seemed pleasant. Tolerable, anyway.

Tears welled in Wren's eyes. She blinked them away, unsure if Isaac was watching her. He had already seen her cry once. Maybe twice. If he were anything like her siblings and cousins—like his siblings and cousins—he would look down on her for the display of weakness. She had to be strong.

She had to do something.

And now was the perfect time. The rotten egg stench had faded. For the moment, it appeared they were unguarded. If they could break free from the chairs, they could escape.

She tugged at the clamps. "How do these open?"

Isaac didn't respond.

Wren's legs were still secured to the chair, but by stretching her arms as far as she could, she managed to tap his shoulder. "Isaac, how do these restraints open?"

"Huh? Oh." He glanced over his shoulder at the opening where the voracan guards used to be. Apparently coming to the same conclusion Wren had—that they were alone for the moment—he said, "There's a small, perfectly round hole. I think the voracans must have a key that fits."

Wren hadn't seen a key on Mine when it had freed her arms, or on any of the other voracans. And, in her admittedly limited experience, keyholes weren't exactly so perfectly round.

But a hole designed for a quill tip might be.

The quill she'd snapped off Mine still lay on the floor. She reached down and grabbed it. "Where are the holes?"

"On the sides, near the metal seam. Why?"

This time Wren was the one who didn't respond. She didn't think any voracans were nearby, but she could have been wrong. There was no point in announcing her escape plans.

Her eyes were useless, but her fingers felt for the hole. When she found it, she stuck the quill inside. The clamp sprang open.

A scream of joy tried to burst from her throat, but she swallowed it down. She wasn't out yet. There were three more clamps. Each opened as easily as the first. She stood.

In the red dimness, Isaac gaped at her. He looked more surprised than happy. Wren suspected he'd assumed she would fail, but she'd shown him. Once she finished rescuing him, she'd show everyone who ever doubted her.

Using the quill, she opened his clamps.

"Do you know the way out of here?" she whispered.

"Yeah. Kind of. We have to—" He stopped. "Someone's coming. Use that device."

She pushed a button, and it turned on.

"Why isn't anything happening?" Isaac whispered. "The voracan's still coming."

Wren didn't see it, but she'd take Isaac's word for it. "I don't know." She pressed the other button, the one that controlled the settings. "Sit down. Pretend you're still stuck in the chair."

The voracan was close enough for her to see—and smell—now, which meant it was very near indeed.

Isaac did his best to look uncomfortable, as if he were still strapped into the machine with hard metal clamps. It wasn't difficult. After spending so long sitting in the rigid chair, he truly was uncomfortable, despite his newfound freedom.

A voracan—not Mine—stood at the main entrance, examining the room. It saw heat and electricity. Could it see the way Isaac's heart thumped in his chest? Could it sense the way his tail rose in excitement?

No, it couldn't. Or, if it could, it did not comprehend the meaning of these things—that the hope of escape had energized Isaac. It left.

Preferring to err on the side of caution, Isaac kept quiet and unmoving for several more minutes.

Next to him, Wren did the same—for a little while, anyway. Then she started fidgeting. "I can't get the device to work," she whispered. "Justin said it might take some trial and error to find the right setting."

"Justin?"

"Yeah, Justin, your friend. He made the device for me."

That didn't make any sense. "How do you know Justin?" Isaac asked. "And how does he know about the voracans? I didn't tell him anything."

"I did."

"So he knows? About me?" Isaac realized they had more urgent problems to deal with, but this frightened him more than anything else.

"I had to tell him." There was a defensive edge to Wren's voice. "He'd already seen the voracans, and I needed help rescuing you. I tried telling my clan, but Iron was too busy talking about war to listen."

"So it's true," Isaac said glumly. "The clepsits and humans are going to wage war, and once both sides are weakened, the voracans will conquer what's left of the surface."

And it was his fault. If he'd remembered to leave his light on, the voracans wouldn't have been able to take him. Their plan would have failed, and he'd be playing with his new friends, who would be blissfully ignorant of what he was. But his secret was out, and everything was ruined.

"Unless we get you to the headquarters and prove that the voracans are behind all of this." Wren fiddled with the device, a rectangular thing with two buttons and an antenna. "I'm not sure I can get this thing to work. We didn't have time to test it. Can we get out of here without being seen?"

"Yeah. I think so." Isaac stood and pushed at the rock wall, warmed by the lamp, but it didn't move. It looked solid, but his fingers found thin lines that confirmed it was not. "There's a door, but I don't know how to open it."

With her left hand—the one not holding the device—Wren felt the wall. "There's an indentation here. I think it's like the ones on the clamps." She took Mine's broken quill. The tip slid into the tiny indentation in the wall. Something clicked, and the previously hidden door opened.

Isaac and Wren hurried into the secret passageway.

Not wanting any voracans to follow them, Isaac pushed the door shut behind them.

Darkness reigned. Isaac stretched out his arms to feel his way through the impenetrable blackness.

Something touched his shoulder. He jumped. A voracan had caught him!

But no—the thing touching his shoulder was soft. It squeezed his arm. He took a deep breath. It was only Wren's hand.

"Where are we going?" she whispered. "I can't see anything. Where are we?"

He took her hand in his and led her forward. "This way," he said, hoping he sounded more confident than he felt.

The ground sloped downward for a while before leveling out. They had to be walking underneath the regular tunnels. For a long time, the narrow passage only gave them two options—forward or backward—but then the passage forked, and Isaac had to make a decision.

"Why are we stopping?" Wren asked. "Is something wrong?"

"No." If these secret passages mirrored the tunnels above, they needed to go left. If the secret passages didn't mirror the tunnels above, he had no idea what to do. He went left. Wren, whose hand he still held, followed.

The temperature rose, sending beads of perspiration dripping down Isaac's brow. Sweat moistened his palms, but when he tried to let go of Wren's hand, she gripped his tighter.

The narrow passageway widened. They'd entered a large room. Isaac knew it was large because he could finally see, though the space was far from bright. In the center of the room sat an infrared lamp, much larger than the ones that marked doors. Heat radiated from it.

"What are these?" Wren asked, pointing at the things that surrounded the red lamp: hundreds and hundreds of black lumps that ranged from the size of a golf ball to the size of a basketball. The larger ones had spikes protruding from the center.

"I don't know." He'd found two broken quills on the ground, and he used one to prod the closest lump. It blinked. "They're voracans! They must be babies."

"Baby . . . voracans . . . all of them?"

"I think so." He paused.

Wren looked at the voracan babies and shuddered. "What do we do now?"

"Keep going." He pointed to a corridor up ahead.

"But what about the babies?" Wren gestured to one of them with her shoe. It looked like she was about to kick it. "They're going to try to kill us. We have to stop them."

The large red lamp produced more heat than light. Wren couldn't see anything more than a few feet in front of her, and even that required her to strain her eyes. At least she was out of the pitch-black passageways.

She couldn't see Isaac very well, but she knew he was staring at her. She could feel it.

"What do you mean, the babies are going to kill us?" he asked.

"They're the enemy." The voracans were trying to start a war. They were succeeding. According to Isaac, if they won, they would try to seize control of the surface and treat the surviving humans and clepsits as livestock.

Iron and Aurora called human power hungry and violent. Aurora always meant it as an insult, but Iron sometimes said it like it was a good thing—something necessary for survival. What if he was right? What if violence sometimes served a purpose?

"They're not the enemy," Isaac said. "They're babies. They haven't done anything to us. They haven't done anything at all."

"Not yet, but they'll grow up. Then they'll want to strap us into machines and drain our marrow just like their parents do. What do you think these babies eat? How many humans and clepsits will it take to feed them?"

"They haven't done anything," Isaac repeated. "Could you really hurt them?"

Why wouldn't she be able to? Because she was human, with poor eyesight, a clumsy gait, and slow reflexes? Maybe she couldn't hunt rabbits and marmots the way her siblings and cousins did, but that didn't mean she was useless. She could rescue Isaac. She could defeat the enemy. One generation of them, anyway. Then, for once, the clepsits would accept her as an equal—more than an equal. They'd probably praise her as a hero. Even Iron would be impressed. Especially Iron. "The voracans want a war, and wars always have casualties. We have to."

"We don't have to do anything. And not all the voracans like those chairs." Isaac started walking away. "Do what you want. I'm going to look for an exit."

"*Look for.*" Meaning he didn't know where it was. He hadn't known about the voracan nursery, either; finding it had obviously surprised him as much as it'd surprised her. He acted as if he knew what he was doing, but he had no clue. She was the rescuer, the champion, the hero.

Isaac disappeared into the dark passageway. Wren stayed behind, staring at the voracan babies.

She had never killed anything before.

One of the babies started to rock back and forth, using its undeveloped quills to push it left, then right, then left again. When it rolled too far in one direction, it crashed into another baby, which started rocking back and forth, too. They gurgled, and it sounded like laughter.

Wren smiled before she could stop herself.

She gave herself a mental scolding. The babies weren't cute. They were voracans, and that meant they were scary. Disgusting. Horrible. They just seemed sort of cute because of their small size. And they weren't laughing. Voracans didn't laugh—not as far as she knew, anyway. The burbling sound might have meant they were hungry. They were the enemy, no matter how small and innocent they appeared.

And enemies had to be stopped.

Wren needed a method that wouldn't involve touching—or looking at—the things.

One of the babies rolled onto her foot. Back and forth it swayed, gurgling happily, apparently trying to get Wren to roll with it and the others.

She closed her eyes. Maybe it would be easier that way.

It wasn't. No matter how she tried to steel herself, she couldn't work up the nerve.

Iron and Aurora made it sound as though all humans possessed some maniacally violent strength, but Wren clearly lacked such a trait. She couldn't hurt the voracan babies any more than she could have hurt the clepsit hatchlings.

She ran out of the room.

Coney stuck to the shadows, although unless his aunt or uncle happened by, it probably wasn't necessary on the upper levels. No one was paying attention to him, not with everything else that was happening. The imprisonment of humans and anyone who supported them. The evacuation of the surrounding town. The large, menacing machines that rolled past the building. The talk of war on everyone's lips.

No one cared about a clepsit boy taking food from the kitchen.

They would have cared if they saw him sneaking

down to the lower levels, but he was too careful for that.

Cheese filled his pockets. Sausages and rolls stuffed his shirt. He took as much as he could carry and wished he could take more. The guards were barely feeding the prisoners. With such an excess of food around, Coney didn't understand it. They threw out pounds upon pounds of food every day, so why should anyone go hungry?

He distributed the food among the prisoners, human and clepsit alike.

"Thank you," Mr. Read said. He smiled sadly. "I can't get over how much you look like Isaac. Has anyone said anything about him?"

Mr. and Mrs. Read still thought Isaac might be alive. No one else did. "Sorry."

"What about Wren?" Mrs. Read asked.

"Sorry." From what Coney gathered, no one had seen her since she left the burrow. No one was even looking for her.

Maybe she'd arrived at the headquarters, seen what was happening, and hightailed it out of there.

Well, *hightail* wasn't quite the right word. She was human, so she didn't have a tail—certainly not a big one that went straight up when she was scared or ex-

cited. That expression obviously only worked for clepsits, but Coney had always thought of Wren as one of
the clan, despite their differences.

"I'm proud of you," Breeze said. She shared a cell
with Bronco and the other human sympathizers. Coney hated to see his parents in prison, but there was
nothing he could do, not without risking their lives.
Even if they got out of the cell, they'd never escape
the building.

"Have you learned anything that might help us?"
Bronco asked.

"Maybe." He had heard rumors about Iron. Nothing substantial enough to share. "I'll keep listening."

Breeze's tail slid between the bars and brushed
against Coney's. "Be careful."

"I will." Coney's ears perked at approaching footsteps. "I have to hide, but I'll return."

He'd try, anyway.

The farther Wren got from the voracan nursery, the darker the corridor became. "Isaac! Isaac, where are you?"

"Straight ahead. Come to the sound of my voice."

"Can't you come here?" She couldn't see anything. He may have been as lost as she was, but he seemed to have an easier time navigating the darkness.

"No. I've found a door. Come this way. It's okay. You're almost here." He kept talking like that until his voice grew louder and closer, and finally his hand grabbed hers. "This should lead somewhere near the room with the machines."

"Okay. I—I didn't do it. I didn't hurt them."

"Good." He sounded relieved. "Ready?"

He opened the door to a dimly lit corridor.

Before, Isaac had said he needed to find an exit. Was he still searching? Were they still lost? She looked at Isaac, whose face radiated confidence when he thought she was looking but fell into an expression of confusion and concern when he thought she wasn't. At least the red lamps in this corridor made it possible for her to see again, if only a little.

"This way," Isaac whispered. He was holding two quills that he must have found on the ground.

Wren had Mine's quill as well as the electro-noception device—not that it would do any good if she couldn't figure out the right setting. She doubted that Isaac actually knew which way to go, but she followed him anyway. She didn't know, either.

A loud humming emanated from somewhere farther down the corridor. A smile lit up Isaac's face. He took a deep breath before breaking into a run. Despite being tired and sore, Wren had no choice but to match his speed. The humming grew louder. By the time they stopped running, it was almost deafening.

Wren stared at the room with wide eyes. It was even larger than the largest human room she'd seen.

There were hundreds of machines, hundreds of weapons, and hundreds of chairs designed to steal marrow.

"Mine!" Isaac gasped.

Wren didn't understand. Something was his? What was his? Then she saw the voracan chasing after them. Mine. The monster that was, according to Isaac, okay.

"We can fight it," Wren said. Even if she couldn't get the device to work, the voracan would be outnumbered two to one. And though she'd felt bad about trying to hurt the babies, this was different. This voracan had strapped her to a chair. This voracan had threatened to drain her marrow. She'd have no remorse when it came to fighting this monster.

She still didn't see why Isaac thought the thing was okay.

Shaking his head, Isaac pointed to the large machines that sat beyond the chairs. "We need one of those."

He ran. Not wanting to be left behind, Wren ran, too.

Behind them, so did Mine.

Isaac ran the fastest. He arrived at the machine first. Using the quill he'd picked up, he opened the door and hopped inside.

When Wren reached the machine a moment later,

she hesitated. She was out of breath, and her side hurt from the exertion, but that wasn't what gave her pause. The voracans built machines that hurt humans and clepsits. She had no desire to climb inside one.

Isaac extended a hand to help her. When she didn't accept it, he said, "It's a tank, but with a drill on top. I think it can tunnel a path to the surface."

The surface. That meant escape. Wren took his hand, but too late. Mine had caught up to them. Its quills swiped at Wren's legs, and she fell. She turned just in time to see a large quill shooting toward her face. Her fingers frantically pushed the button on the electro-no-ception device, though she hadn't yet managed to find the right setting and doubted she would succeed in the mere fractions of a second remaining before the sharp quill struck her.

"Please," Isaac pleaded. "Let us go. Please."

The quill froze. Isaac pulled Wren into the tank.

With Wren safe inside, Isaac shut the tank's door. "It stopped," she said. "It was going to strike me, and it stopped. The electro-no-ception device must have worked."

"Maybe," Isaac said, but he wasn't convinced. "The device is supposed to disrupt the voracans' senses, but Mine didn't seem confused. I think it stopped on purpose."

The tank was shaped like a squat cylinder, about six feet in diameter and five feet in height. It had been pieced together from metal scraps, the ragged seams easy to identify. In two places—one on the ceiling and one on the side—thick panels of dark but transparent plastic, similar to tinted car windows, replaced the metal. Isaac wondered at their purpose. The tint must have been there to protect the voracans from sunlight when they ventured up to the surface. The voracans wouldn't have wanted to see outside, though, not in the manner of humans or clepsits. Perhaps the voracans could sense heat and electricity easier through plastic than they could through metal.

Regardless, the two panels provided Isaac with a view outside, and he was happy for them.

Wren, who'd been on the metal floor until then, stood. Had she been any taller, she would have had to stoop. "How do we operate this thing?"

"I don't know." There was no steering wheel. There were, however, three small holes below the plastic panels, similar to the ones that opened the doors and unlocked the clamps. Isaac stuck a quill inside one.

The tank vibrated. Through the upper plastic panel, Isaac watched the drill spin.

Wren pointed to the second hole. "What does this one do?"

To answer her own question, she stuck her quill in. As she shifted the quill, the machine moved forward, backward, left, and right in response. When she inserted a quill into the third hole, the machine lifted itself up, and the drill scraped against the ceiling. She removed the quill, and the machine thudded to the ground.

"I think the quill becomes a sort of lever, like the controls in a helicopter or a joystick in an old video game," Isaac said, before remembering that Wren might never have seen a helicopter, a joystick, or a video game. "Whichever way you move the quill, the tank moves, too."

After some experimentation, she began to move the tank forward.

"We need to go up," Isaac said. He couldn't navigate his way through the labyrinthine voracan tunnels, but he knew the general direction home. "Not forward. Straight up."

"Not yet." Wren squinted through the plastic panel. "The other tanks are too big to destroy, but I think I can take out the chairs. Hold on."

There was nothing to hold on to. There weren't even seats, much less seat belts. The floor was rough in some spots and smooth and slippery in others, and the jagged seams and barbs that jutted up where the metal had been welded together threatened to cut anyone who wasn't careful. The machine wasn't built to be comfortable or safe.

It wasn't built to operate as a steamroller, either. It was supposed to dig tunnels to the surface, not flatten metal beneath it. But the large and heavy design meant it got the job done. Under Wren's control, the tank heaved itself over the rows of chairs.

Most of the chairs were simply crushed under the weight, but others burst apart, their pieces ricocheting off nearby machines. A chunk of metal flew straight at the plastic panel that Isaac and Wren peered through. Isaac ducked, desperately attempting to protect his head and neck with his arms. He braced himself for impact.

The plastic cracked, but the metal chunk didn't breach it.

And Wren didn't stop. She maneuvered the tank back and forth along each row until she had destroyed every single chair.

It probably wouldn't make a difference. Mine had said this was only one of the voracans' many arsenals. Nevertheless, the more chairs they destroyed, the happier Isaac was.

He didn't see Mine anywhere. The voracan must

have fled as soon as they'd entered the tank. Would the others know it had let them go? And if so, what would happen? Isaac hated to think that Mine might be punished for its kindness.

He also hated to think that the voracans, having discovered the escape, were forming a new plan of attack. Any second now, a horde of them might burst into the room and tear the tank apart.

Wren might have been thinking the same thing.

"How do we get out of here?" she asked, apparently satisfied that she had destroyed as much of the voracans' arsenal as she could.

"We go up."

She frowned. "Straight up? I thought you knew about a path we could take out of here."

"We don't need one. The tank will drill the way for us." At least, that was what Isaac assumed would happen. He hadn't had the opportunity to test his theory, and the voracans—even Mine—weren't exactly willing to share such information. He couldn't imagine any other purpose the drills that topped the tanks could serve.

Wren went back to experimenting with the controls. She reinserted the third quill into the third hole, and the tank lurched up. The drill hit the dirt ceiling, and dirt poured down. "It's working!"

The tank plummeted to the ground even though Wren had not removed the third quill.

Isaac yelped at the impact, which had knocked him down. The cracks in the plastic panel widened slightly, but otherwise the machine had survived the crash intact.

"What happened?" Wren had fallen in the crash, too, but now she was back at the controls, trying again.

"No!" Isaac tried to stand, failed, and ended up crawling over to Wren and the controls. "We can't go straight up."

"But you said to!"

"I know. I was wrong." If they went straight up, they would have nothing below them, and gravity would yank them back down. "We need to move at an angle. There has to be something beneath us or we'll fall again."

Wren thought about this for a moment. "Okay, I think I can do that." She directed the tank toward the nearest wall. Once there, she maneuvered it up and forward, into the earth at a steep slope. Dirt poured in through the cracked plastic panel.

They were really doing it! They were digging their way out.

They couldn't see where they were going anymore—there was too much dirt in the way—but it didn't seem to matter. Every second carried them farther and farther from the voracans. If they kept going up, eventually they'd reach the surface, and then they could figure out exactly where they were and how to get home.

Assuming they could make it that far. Dirt kept pouring in through the cracked panel. Soon, it covered the entire floor. Good thing they weren't trying to drive the tank through water, as they surely would have drowned by now. Even the dirt, which seemed harmless enough in small quantities, worried Isaac. If they kept tunneling like this for long enough, the dirt would bury them alive.

How far was it to the surface? A mile? Two?

"Where are we going to come up?" Wren asked.

"I don't know." Hopefully it would be in Salmon City, or at least somewhere nearby. Tired and sore, he didn't want to have to walk far, but he would if he had to. In the long run, it didn't matter where they surfaced.

Unless . . . unless they surfaced in the middle of

someone's house. Or in a park where kids were playing. Or a school. Or a doctor's office. Or anywhere that wasn't the middle of nowhere. They were barreling forward with no clue where they were headed or what damage they might cause. "Stop! We have to stop!"

Wren did not stop the tank. "Why? What's wrong?"

"We have to figure out where we're going."

She frowned. "But how? We can't see anything."

"I don't know. We have to figure something out." But it was too late. The tank increased speed as the drill broke through the surface. Dirt stopped pouring through the cracks. "Stop the tank! Stop the tank!"

Wren pulled on one of the quills, which made the tank move backward and to one side. When she moved the quill again, the tank started spinning. Finally, she tore all three quills from their holes. The tank came to a halt.

Isaac didn't hear any screams. That was a good sign. He grabbed one of the quills and used it to pop the door open. He and Wren jumped out.

A cow stared at them from behind a fence. Several other cows grazed nearby. They had surfaced in a field, otherwise empty. It was daylight, but thanks to a heavy cloud cover, he couldn't tell what time it was. A few refreshing raindrops sprinkled down.

"We're somewhere on the edge of town," Isaac said. He'd seen areas like this when his family had driven into Salmon City. "We'll have to walk."

"I have a better idea." Wren took out a phone that looked very much like the one Isaac owned. She fumbled with the buttons for a minute or so before finding what she needed. "Hi, Sara," she yelled, loud enough to startle the cows. "Can you hear me?" Her voice became softer. "Oh, sorry. It's me, Wren. Isaac is with me. Can you come get us?"

Following Sara's instructions, Wren used something called GPS to find their location. Then Sara promised that someone would come to help. At this point, the phone stopped carrying Sara's voice. Wren shook it a few times, and said hello a few more times. Getting no response, she decided the conversation was over and put the phone back in her pocket.

Isaac asked, "Who were you talking to?"

"Sara." Wren sat down next to him.

"Sara? She knows, too? What about Ryan? Did you tell him?" It seemed as though everyone had learned his secrets.

"Yeah. All three of them saw the voracan, and some arboreal clepsits that had been sniffing around your house. And all three of them were there when Justin offered to make the electro-no-ception device." She glanced at the device. "Maybe he can figure out why it didn't work."

"Yeah, maybe. But, uh, how much did you tell them about me?"

"As much as I could. Like I said, I needed their help. No one else was trying to help my birth parents. Your parents. And no one else was looking for you. I couldn't rescue you on my own."

Isaac nodded. He looked just like Bronco when he made that gesture, and it reminded Wren how much she missed her family. Her mother, father, and Coney, anyway.

"Did they think it was gross?" he asked. "What I am, I mean. The tail and everything."

"No. They thought it was cool. Listen, you can relax, okay? They promised not to tell anyone. And they seemed pretty certain no one would believe them if they tried." Wren didn't understand why Isaac was so upset. "Aren't you happy to have someone you can confide in? And to be out of the voracans' lair?"

"Yeah. Of course. It's just—they know." Isaac

ripped a few blades of grass from the ground. "It's okay. I wouldn't have been able to stay here long anyway. They were only temporary friends."

Temporary friends? "Maybe human society is different, but in the clepsit burrows, friends are family. You can't get away from them." No matter how desperately Wren might have wanted to.

"Human society *is* different. At least it is for me. Once, my tail slipped out while I was playing, and we had to move early. We'll have to move again now." He bit his lip. "Have you seen my parents? Your birth parents? Everyone thinks they hurt me. Are they okay?"

"I think so. They weren't at your house, but that's good. They're probably hiding somewhere. As soon as we get you to the headquarters, show everyone that you're alive, and tell everyone what really happened, they won't have to hide anymore."

Wren didn't mention all the things that could go wrong—that the voracans could leap out of the ground and recapture them or that the war could be too advanced to stop. Isaac, who must have been aware of these possibilities as well, didn't mention them, either.

* * *

A large motored carriage appeared. It stopped, and Sara, Justin, and Ryan hopped out.

"You did it!" Sara hugged Wren, then Isaac, who looked quite startled by the gesture.

"Did the electro-no-ception device work?" Justin asked.

"No, I don't think so." Wren told them how they escaped, omitting the part about the voracan babies. Anyone who heard about that would think she was a monster for wanting to hurt the babies, or a coward for not going through with it. Either way, no one would think she'd done the right thing.

Justin took the device and fiddled with the controls. "It seems all right. Maybe you just couldn't find the right setting."

"Or maybe the voracans' senses don't work the way we thought," Sara said.

Justin nodded. "It's possible. Keep it just in case. I'm working on a second one for us."

Wren put the device back in her pocket. "We need to go to the clepsit rail station. It's at Rose Avenue, number, uh, five-four-six."

They got into the motored carriage. Another person, a little older than the others, sat inside.

"This is Becca," Ryan said. "My sister."

"Your wonderful, kind, generous sister who agreed to drive to the middle of nowhere to pick up your friends. I still don't understand why everyone had to come. I hate driving the minivan. And how did you get out here?" She pointed to the tank. "And what is that?"

"A generous sister wouldn't have made me promise to do her chores for a month," Ryan said. "And you agreed no questions."

"That was before I knew this little trip involved weird machines." She eyed Isaac. "Or children covered with scratches and dirt. You don't look so good. Do you need to go to the hospital?"

"No!" Isaac said. "No doctors."

"His, uh, family doesn't believe in doctors," Sara said. "It's a religious thing."

He nodded.

"Fine, but if you're doing something you're not supposed to, I'm not covering for you. One month of chores isn't enough." Becca addressed Wren. "You have to put on your seat belt."

"What?" Wren looked around, confused, until Ryan helped her fix a piece of material around her lap and chest. "Sorry, I've never been in a motored carriage before."

"A motored carriage?" Becca asked. "Do you mean a car?"

"No questions," Ryan reminded her.

Wren hoped no one minded a question or two from her. "Have you heard anything new about Pacis?" she asked.

"Not much. The cl—" Sara stopped, glancing at Becca. "The, uh, group is still controlling the entire city block, but they haven't issued any demands yet."

"I heard they're some sort of ecoterrorism cell," Becca said. "And they must have some sort of weapon or hostages or something to keep the government from stepping in. My friend Amy thinks they've been mutated by pollution, and that's why they look so weird and why they're angry. And the government is trying to cover up the truth, and that's why there are hardly any official reports."

"That last part is true," Justin said. "There haven't been a lot of official statements. Most of what we see is from reporters sneaking past the barricades or people flying drones overhead."

Wren had never heard of a drone, but if people flew it, she supposed it had to be one of those airplane contraptions humans liked. She'd seen one flying over the burrow once before. Or drones could be a type of balloon. Humans liked those, too.

Regardless, it was good that most humans didn't know what was really happening. Someone at the headquarters must have been using their connections to keep everything quiet. If the situation kept deteriorating, though, that wouldn't be possible for much longer.

Ryan handed her a plastic bottle and a perfectly sealed bag. It took a moment for Wren to realize it was water and food—according to the label, potato chips. The chips were satisfyingly crunchy, and although they were too salty for her tastes, she gobbled them down.

Isaac ate the food offered to him, too, and just as quickly.

"Are you sure you don't want to rest here before moving on?" Sara asked. "You could spend the night at my house, Wren. Isaac, you could stay with one of the guys—get some real food, some clean clothes, and a bath. Maybe a gallon of disinfectant. Some of those scratches are pretty bad. What do you think?"

Isaac shook his head.

Wren, remembering that humans used the gesture to mean no, shook her head, too. "We need to hurry."

Becca dropped them off near the clepsit rail station, where Sara, Justin, and Ryan got out to hug them goodbye and wish them good luck. They wanted to see the rails, but Becca kept making her motored carriage—her car—honk like a goose, and they said this meant they had to go. Wren and Isaac had to continue their journey alone.

Which was fine, Wren thought. The rails wouldn't be so bad now that she had company. Compared to the voracan lair, it would be luxurious. The hard part was over.

All they had to do now was stop a war.

Isaac didn't mind the hardness of the clepsit carriage or the sharpness of its angles, but it wouldn't have killed the designer to toss in a few cushions.

He did, however, mind the darkness. The paint that covered the rails glowed, but not brightly enough to ward off voracans. "We should keep the device on," he told Wren. "If the voracans attack, we might be able to get it to work."

"I thought about it," she said, "but Justin said it could run out of power, and we'd have to find the right setting, anyway. We'll turn it on if the voracans attack, but I don't think they will. They're probably still recovering from our escape and fixing all the chairs we broke, and I don't think they know where we are. Try to relax. We're okay."

Isaac surprised himself by smiling. Wren was right. They *were* okay, compared to how they'd been just a little while ago, anyway. Problems remained, undoubtedly—the threat of war, the accusations against his parents—but now that he was free, he could fix everything.

And, although it shouldn't have mattered so much, not with everything else that had been happening, he couldn't help but smile at his newfound chance to make friends. Not just temporary friends. *Real* friends. They knew who he was—what he was— and they didn't laugh at him or run away.

Maybe Wren would be his friend, too. More than that. She would be family. He couldn't wait to meet the rest of his family.

"How many siblings do you—I—have?" he asked.

"Three brothers," Wren said. "Coney, Colt, and Taurus. And one sister, Kit, and a ton of cousins. We all live together, so it's pretty crowded."

"Whoa!" The information he gleaned from the occasional comment his mother let slip led him to suspect his family was large, but he hadn't realized how large. "What are clepsit houses like?" They must have been huge.

"Clepsits don't live in houses. Northern clepsits live in underground burrows. I'm not sure about the others. I think arboreal clepsits live in tree houses, and the aquatic clepsits live underwater, of course. We don't ever see them, though."

Isaac's eyes widened as he imagined this. Tree houses. Burrows. It would be like a permanent camping trip. He'd miss his TV and video games, but otherwise it sounded amazing.

"What about your—my parents, the Reads? What are they like?" Wren asked.

Isaac smiled. "Wonderful. Dad bakes the best cookies ever, and Mom knows everything about everything." His smile faded. "I hope they're okay. They must be worried about me."

He was worried about them, too.

"They'll be fine, as soon as we get to the headquarters." Wren yawned. "I'm going to try to sleep. You should do the same."

Between the way the carriage rocked and the way his mind raced, Isaac thought he'd never manage to sleep. He was still thinking this as he drifted off.

***

The carriage stopped. Isaac woke up. "How many more stations are there?" he asked.

They'd been traveling southeast for a while now, and every time they came to a station, they had to hoist themselves and the carriage up using a pulley system. His arms still ached from the last time. He didn't know how Wren had done it on her own before. She had to be very strong for her size. Brave, too. He bet everyone in her family loved and admired her. Would they ever love and admire him as much?

"None." There was tension in Wren's voice.

Still groggy from his nap, Isaac took a moment to process the meaning of this. There were no more stops. They had arrived at the headquarters. "That's great!"

"Yeah," Wren said, sounding less convinced. "Except for the war that's starting above us."

"That's why we're here. To stop it."

They hauled themselves up on the manual elevator. When they reached the surface, they found two clepsits staring at them.

Clepsits! Actual clepsits! Isaac had never seen one before, except, of course, on frequent occasions involving a mirror. These weren't the northern type that he belonged to, but he could identify them from the descriptions his mother had given him. They belonged to the large, furry Antarctic group.

Very large. Very armed, too. They both had large spears, which they raised in a way that came off as rather threatening.

Probably because they didn't know who he was. "I'm Isaac. Isaac Read. My mother, Faun Read, is the North American ambassador." Or should he have said his father, Bronco of Snow, was the ambassador?

One of the clepsits said, "Isaac Read is dead."

"No, I'm not. That was a lie." Obviously.

"The Reads were telling the truth," Wren said. "They didn't hurt Isaac. The voracans kidnapped him and framed the Reads. They're trying to start a war. We need to speak to someone in charge."

"Fine," said the same clepsit. "This way."

They did not put down their spears. In fact, they kept them pointed directly at Wren and Isaac.

* * *

Isaac did not know the man who stood before him. How could he have known him when, aside from the two spear-carrying men, he had never met another clepsit in his life? He could assume, though, from the size of the office and the deference of the spear carriers, that this man held a role of great importance.

A window offered a view of the city streets, all of which were oddly deserted. Helicopters hovered in the distance.

"Iron," Wren said. "What are you doing here?"

"All first fathers and mothers were called to the headquarters as soon as war became inevitable. A better question would be: what are *you* doing here?"

"This is Isaac." She gestured to him. "He's not dead. The Reads never hurt him. The voracans kidnapped him to frame the Reads to start a war, and I rescued him. Who do we need to talk to? Who's in charge here?"

Iron smiled. "I am. Someone had to take control of the situation."

"Then you have to call off the fighting!"

Iron's smile remained in place. "Why would I do that?"

"Because Isaac's alive! There's no reason to fight."

"What about land, resources, power? There's always a reason to fight. As a human, you should know this." He turned to the two Antarctic clepsits. "Put them in one of the cells. Throw away the key."

"I don't understand," Wren said.

But Isaac understood perfectly.

Because right then, a voracan tank rolled past the window and down the otherwise empty street.

Wren had imagined meeting her birth parents before. She'd pictured them coming to her burrow, and she'd pictured herself going to their home. At the time, she'd had no idea what a human dwelling looked like, but from Aurora's many rants, she'd understood it had to be luxuriously warm and comfortable. Whenever Iron refused to waste more wood on the fire, Wren had daydreamed about the happy times she'd eventually share with her human parents.

She'd never guessed they'd be meeting in adjoining prison cells, separated by thick metal bars.

She recognized them right away. For one thing,

Faun Read's hair was the exact same shade of red as Wren's. She would have known anyway, though, even if Faun Read had been bald. They looked like her parents should. They *felt* like her parents should.

And then there was Isaac referring to them as Mom and Dad. Not letting the bars stop him, he slid his arms through gaps to hug them. Everyone was crying and smiling at once.

Wren was tempted to join the hug, but she stayed back. Despite the biological relationship they shared, she was a stranger.

Besides, she had her own reunion to enjoy. Bronco and Breeze, the parents who had raised her, were there as well. She was glad to see them at first, but that happiness faded quickly. They were locked up, too, stuck in the adjoining cell on the other side.

She hugged them through the bars, just as Isaac had done with his parents. Her mother's tail stroked her hair.

"I found Isaac," she said. "I didn't believe he'd been killed, so I went to his house, and the voracans had taken him, and they took me, too, but we got out."

Her mother and father didn't seem capable of forming a response. Among everyone there, enough tears fell to fill a bath basin.

Then Isaac came over, apparently not as worried about being a stranger to his birth parents. He stared at them with awe in his eyes.

"Isaac," Bronco whispered, and they hugged, their tails entwining.

Wren looked at her human father and mother. They beckoned her forward, and she went to them.

"Thank you," her human father said, embracing her through the bars like he had done with Isaac. "Thank you, thank you, thank you."

"I don't understand," Wren said after they had finished their hugs, spilled more tears than seemed possible, and filled each other in on all that had happened. "Why did Iron send us here? Can't he see that Isaac's okay? That it was all part of a voracan plot?"

"He's working with the voracans," Isaac said. "I saw one of the voracan tanks outside his window, and there was a clepsit inside, looking through the plastic panel. Iron's working with the voracans. Mine—one of the voracans—said the designs for the chair came from someone on the surface. It must have been him."

"That doesn't make sense," Wren said.

"It makes perfect sense," Bronco said. "He's always said that clepsits need to make a power play and take control of the planet. Now he's doing it."

Trying to gain power was one thing, but partnering with the voracans? That was madness. Wren couldn't believe anyone would be so foolish. "The voracans aren't going to share the planet. They want to turn clepsits and humans into a bone marrow factory."

"They're both planning to double-cross each other," Bronco said. "They both think they can win."

"And whichever side wins," Mrs. Read said, "we lose."

* * *

That evening, a clepsit guard carried out the full trash can and, complaining that the trash cans used at the headquarters were too heavy and hurt his back, returned with an empty one. Wren could not find it in herself to feel sorry for him.

He also brought food for everyone. It wasn't much more appealing than what one would expect to find in a trash can. Maybe that was where he'd gotten it.

As a prisoner, Wren received a chunk of stale bread and a bowl of cold bean soup for dinner. It made her miss the food the voracans had given her. Not that she wanted to go back. She'd take the prison cell over the marrow-draining chair any day, even if that chair didn't work yet. Nevertheless, this wasn't quite the improvement she'd been hoping for.

The guard left. Everyone nibbled on their horrible food in silence. Now that the excitement of the reunion had faded, the hopelessness of their situation overwhelmed Wren.

The trash can wobbled.

A head peeked out.

"Coney!" Wren clapped her hands over her mouth. He'd clearly sneaked in there, and she didn't want to give him away. In case the guards outside were listening, she added, in an equally loud voice, "I miss Coney! I hate this place."

Coney climbed out of the trash can. He approached Isaac and, speaking in a whisper, said, "I overheard someone say you were here, but I didn't believe it. Are you really Isaac?"

Isaac nodded.

Coney smiled. "I'm your brother, Coney."

Isaac returned the smile, but it was a sad expression that failed to convey much joy. Wren understood. She was happy to see Coney, just as she'd been delighted to see her parents, but the fact that they were prisoners could not be ignored. Even meeting her human parents hadn't been enough to make her forget her many worries for very long.

What was she supposed to call them, anyway? Mother and Father? Faun and John? Mr. and Mrs. Read? She had no clue.

"I need to get you out of here," Coney continued. "People need to see you."

"That was our original plan," Wren said. "Bring Isaac here, let everyone see that he's alive, that the voracans kidnapped him and blamed his parents to start a war." She gestured to the bars that surrounded her. "It didn't go the way we'd hoped."

"Not everyone is as eager for war as Iron," Coney said. "If they see Isaac, I think some clepsits might help. I think Aurora might help."

Wren was sure she'd heard that wrong. "Aurora? Why would Aurora help any of us? We're all humans or human sympathizers, and she hates us." It was probably her idea to form an alliance with the voracans.

"It's true," Breeze admitted. "I always hoped she would change her mind, but she never did."

Coney looked over his shoulder. They'd been making a lot of noise, so he was probably worried that the guards would be coming to check on them. They weren't. "I've heard rumors about her, about how she's been fighting with Iron. I think we should try talking to her."

If Aurora was fighting with Iron, it was probably because she thought Iron was being too kind to the humans, not locking up enough of them. Were they really going to pin all their hopes on her?

Then again, what other option did they have?

Isaac had always known there was a great deal of tension between humans and clepsits. After all, that was why ambassadors were needed and why they had to exchange children. The whole point was to ease the tension by increasing cross-species understanding.

But he hadn't expected so much animosity within his own family. His own uncle had thrown his parents—both sets—in prison, and Wren didn't seem to think his aunt was much nicer.

He wanted to get to know his birth parents better, but honestly, he was a little afraid of what he might learn if he kept asking questions. Did they have dark secrets, too? Besides, the prison cell hardly seemed like the best place for a family reunion.

"I don't understand," he said. "You want me to go see Aurora, but how am I supposed to do that? I'm locked in a cell."

Coney removed a key from his pants pocket. "I can get you out. Then I'll take your place, and you'll sneak up to her room. Aurora is staying in three-oh-six."

Wren reached for the key, but with the metal bars in her way, she couldn't get close enough to grab them. "If you have the keys, why don't you just free us all?"

Coney stepped away from the cell, putting the keys even farther from her grasping fingers. "I get around by sneaking in trash cans, under food carts, and behind curtains, but I'm one small clepsit. Iron would notice if all his prisoners suddenly escaped. You'd never get far. Security's too tight. Iron has two guards outside, plus more throughout the building. And he has the building surrounded."

"Won't the guards notice that you're not me?" Isaac asked. They looked alike, but not identical.

"We'll trade clothes, and I'll stay in the corner. I don't think they'll notice, not right away." After checking over his shoulder a couple of times, Coney slid the key into the lock on the cell door. It opened.

"I'm going with Isaac," Wren said.

"You can't," Coney said. "There's no one to replace you."

"We'll put a bunch of clothes, trash—whatever we can find—under the blanket on my bed and make it look like I'm lying there. The guards don't pay much attention to us. They won't notice—at least not for a while." She crossed her arms. "I don't trust Aurora, and I'm not letting Isaac go to see her alone."

Coney sighed. "Okay, but I don't think it's a good idea."

He wasn't the only one. Nevertheless, Isaac was happy for the company.

***

Isaac and Wren couldn't sneak out in trash cans, not unless they wanted to wait a couple of days while the trash can filled. So they decided to go out the main door. Where the two Antarctic clepsits stood guard.

Mr. Read provided the necessary distraction. "My heart!" he shouted. "I need help."

The guards didn't come, although they must have heard him.

A little while later, they tried a new approach. One of the guards was bringing them breakfast or lunch or whatever meal was due. All the food was the same, and the windowless cells made keeping track of time difficult.

"Quick! Bronco! Faun! Hide it!" Breeze said, in a very loud whisper. A stage whisper: the sort an actor in a play would use so that the audience could hear.

Bronco and Mrs. Read made a show of hiding something—actually nothing—under their beds.

"Valor!" the guard yelled, and the other guard—whose name must have been Valor—entered the room. "They're hiding something. You search his cell. I'll search hers." He pointed to Bronco and Mrs. Read. While the two guards tore the beds apart in pursuit of the imaginary contraband, Isaac and Wren slipped away.

They were at the elevator when they heard someone moan.

It was a horrible sound, the type that could be made only by someone in pain. By someone being beaten by a guard. Isaac wondered who it was—

Bronco or Mrs. Read, probably, but possibly one of the others. Whoever it was, it was someone trying to help Wren and him.

A muffled cry followed a second moan.

Wren stopped. "We have to go back," she whispered.

45

Wren winced at each moan, her mind providing unwanted images to go with the wretched sounds. She pictured her father on the ground while big furry feet kicked and stomped. Or Mrs. Read cowering in a corner while spears cut her flesh.

Together, maybe they could overpower the guards. Even if they were at least five times larger—and stronger—than her and Isaac combined. Still, they could try.

"We have to go back," she repeated.

"No," Isaac said. "We have to find Aurora. Otherwise, things will get a lot worse than this."

Wren hesitated. She wanted to go back, to fight and help her family. She did not want to try to convince Aurora—Aurora of all people!—to fight for her.

But Isaac was right. They had to stick to the plan.

She reached forward to press the button next to the elevator. She'd seen the guards use it before, when they'd escorted her and Isaac to see Iron, so she knew it made the elevator doors open.

Isaac grabbed her wrist to stop her. "There'll be cameras. We need to take the stairs."

He led them to a door marked EXIT. Wren frowned. They wanted to stay in the building, not exit it. Isaac seemed to know what he was doing, though. She never would've thought about cameras, which she figured humans only used to take pictures of friends and family that they could put in photo albums later. Why would there be cameras in an elevator?

Clepsits currently controlled the headquarters, which were situated atop a clepsit rail station, but the building itself was human through and through. And Wren knew very little when it came to humans.

The moans and cries faded. Which was good—except it meant that the guards would return any second. She followed Isaac.

The door opened to a dimly lit stairwell. Every step

they took echoed against the concrete surroundings. They tiptoed as quickly and quietly as they could.

"Do you still have the device?" Isaac asked.

"Yes." Wren took it out of her pocket. She didn't smell the telltale stench of rotten eggs, but the lack of strong light made her uneasy. There were voracan machines around. Were there voracans, too? "Should I turn it on? Do you see a voracan?"

"No. Just have it ready."

She held it in her hands, though her sweaty palms threatened to let it slip from her grasp. To prevent this, she had to keep switching off from her right hand to her left hand and back again.

The steps seemed endless. They didn't move like the ones at the mall she visited when she was looking for Isaac. Here, her legs had to do all the work.

They came to a door. "Should we go out?" Wren asked.

"No. Not yet."

So they kept walking. When they reached the second door, Wren repeated her question, and Isaac repeated his answer. *"Not yet."* At the third door, Wren didn't bother asking.

"This is the door," Isaac said.

It looked exactly like the other doors to Wren. "How do you know?"

"We were in the basement, and Aurora's in room three-oh-six, which must be on the third floor. So this is the door."

Oh. More numbers. Humans sure did like them.

Isaac opened the door a crack and peered out. Then he closed the door. "Someone's there."

They waited in silence. After a while, Isaac tried again. "The coast is clear. Let's go."

46

The door to room 306 opened, which struck Isaac as too easy. Shouldn't it have been locked? It might have been a trap. The guards had overheard their plans, and now they stood ready to attack the escaped prisoners.

Or maybe, because the building—the entire neighborhood—was supposed to be secure, Aurora didn't feel it was necessary to worry about her room. Or perhaps clepsits never used locks. They lived in burrows, after all. Locks must have seemed rather alien.

Isaac plowed ahead, with Wren beside him.

A clepsit woman had been sitting at a small table, but she rose upon hearing the intruders. She was one of the northern clepsits—her hair, skin, and eyes currently dark for the summer. Aurora.

"I'm Isaac," he said, getting right to the point. "My parents didn't hurt me. The voracans did. It was all a plot to start a war. We need your help."

Aurora stared at him for a moment. Then, with strength unexpected from such a small body, she shoved Isaac and Wren in a closet. It was cramped inside since half the space was already taken up by a fold-out ironing board and several pieces of fur clothing.

Aurora pulled the flimsy accordion-style door shut.

"I knew it!" Wren shrieked. "I knew she'd never help—"

Isaac clamped a hand over her mouth. "Shh!"

The door to the room, which was far sturdier than the closet door, banged open and then shut again.

"Hello, Iron," Aurora said, much louder and clearer than seemed natural. "How is everything going?"

"Very well," came Iron's voice, sounding quite pleased. Smug, even. "We have more tanks coming in. I hope to expand clepsit control to the entire city by early next week. I've been talking to clepsits at the

South American and European headquarters, and I think I can convince them to join us."

"Really?" Aurora sounded very close, as if she was standing in front of the closet. "They're willing to work with the voracans?"

"What choice do they have? As bad as the voracans are, the humans are worse. They murdered the boy they were raising as a son. By doing so, they ended the ambassador program—the only thing keeping the peace between us."

"Yes. Yes, so we've been told. And I suppose that leaves us with no choice." She took a deep breath, audible even from inside the closet. "How does lunch sound? I thought we could go down to the dining hall. I just need to do a couple of things first. Why don't you go on ahead of me?"

"I can wait for you here," Iron said.

"But if you go down now, you can order some of that delicious roast duck for me, and it'll be ready when I get there. I'm very hungry, you see. Please."

"All right." The door to the room thudded shut.

Aurora yanked the closet door open, her eyes moist. "You're alive! I can't tell you how happy I am to see you."

Isaac stepped out of the way, sure that Aurora had

to be talking to Wren, her niece. But before he could move more than an inch, Aurora tackled him with a hug. She ignored Wren.

Wren crossed her arms. "We don't have much time."

Aurora released Isaac from her embrace. "It's too dangerous for you to wander around the building. Iron has spies everywhere. I'll keep him out of this room. It shouldn't be too difficult. He's in meetings most of the time anyway."

"Then what?" Isaac asked. "We can't just hide. We need to do something. We need to stop the war."

"Yes, yes, of course. Everyone's uneasy about the alliance with the voracans. They're only going along with Iron's plan because he's convinced them that the humans are plotting against us. Once they see you, they'll know it isn't true. They'll stop backing Iron. He's not powerful enough on his own, not yet."

"So you're going to help us?" Wren asked. "Why? You hate humans. You of all people should jump at the chance to wage war against us."

"Where would that put my sons? Wars require soldiers. And I don't hate humans. It's just that . . . It's just that they're so dirty. And smelly. They're clumsy, greedy, violent, and power obsessed. And they have so many wars! If we start a war, too, we'll hardly be better than them."

Isaac was beginning to understand why Wren disliked her aunt. Nevertheless, it looked like Aurora sincerely wanted to help. And they needed all the help they could get.

"But what about Iron?" Wren persisted. "He's your husband. You're really going to betray him to help me? I don't believe it."

Aurora's face hardened. "Iron betrayed all of us when he began working with the voracans. I only just found out, but he's been doing it in secret for months, perhaps years. He's almost as ambitious as a human. Sometimes I think that's the only reason he paired with me—to become more powerful, the first husband of the clan."

Wren kept her arms crossed. "I still don't believe you'd lie to him to help us."

"Well, you're right. I'm not doing this to help you. I'm doing it to help my children. I need to go now, or he'll wonder where I am. Like I said, I'll try to keep him out of here, but just in case, hide in the closet if anyone enters the room." She gave Isaac—and only Isaac—another hug. "We can't let you disappear again."

Wren still didn't believe her aunt. Aurora only wanted to gain their trust so she could hand them back to Iron. Even if she did help them stop the voracans—which wasn't likely—she'd probably just turn around and do something even worse later.

And humans were not dirty!

"We should leave. If we can sneak out of the building, we should be able to find someone who's not working with Iron."

Isaac's mouth fell open. "Are you joking? We already found someone."

"Aurora? We're better off alone. You don't know her the way I do."

"You don't like her. She doesn't like you. I get it. But Coney said she'd side with us, and he was right. I'm staying."

Wren knew that Coney would never lie to her, but that didn't mean he couldn't be wrong. So what if Aurora had kept them hidden from Iron? That didn't prove anything. She had to be planning something awful. Wren just didn't know what it was.

She supposed she could stick around just long enough to find out. That way, whenever Aurora's plan started to unfold, Wren would be there to stop it. "Fine. We'll stay. But keep your guard up."

They sat on the floor, then on the bed, which was far more comfortable than the ones in the prison cell. Occasionally they sneaked peeks outside the window, always careful to keep themselves hidden behind the curtains, and watched the tanks go past. They didn't see any voracans, but the afternoon sun still beamed brightly enough that they didn't expect to.

The room had a small refrigerator stocked with water, juice, and a box of something that Isaac called lasagna. They helped themselves.

"It's even better hot," Isaac said, but Wren thought

it was delicious cold. Judging by how much he ate, Isaac must have liked it well enough, too.

As the sun crept toward the horizon, Aurora had yet to return.

Eventually, Isaac and Wren grew tired, but sleeping on the bed was too dangerous. Anyone who walked in would see them if they slept there. Instead, they curled up in the closet with a couple of pillows.

It was, without contest, the most comfortable nap Wren had enjoyed in days. She awoke feeling almost refreshed. Isaac was still asleep. She quietly got up and checked the room, which was dark and empty. She turned on a light before returning to the closet.

The door to the room opened. Isaac awoke, and the two remained in the closet.

"What's this all about?" came a voice Wren didn't recognize.

"Where's Iron?" came another. "What's going on, Aurora?"

The closet door opened, revealing Aurora and three other clepsits: a large Antarctic woman, a blue man with webbed fingers, and a green arboreal man. "Come out," Aurora said, extending a hand to help Isaac up and ignoring Wren. "I'd like you to meet Isaac Read. Isaac, these are Speed of Forest and Kelp of Wave, the first fathers of their clans, and Grace of South, the first mother of her clan. Why don't you tell them what you told me?"

He told them. They listened without saying a word.

The arboreal man, Speed, curled his tail into a tight ball vaguely reminiscent of a fist. "We have to stop Iron."

"And the voracans," the blue man, Kelp, agreed.

"How can we?" asked the Antarctic woman, Grace, her white fur bristling. "The city is swarming with them by now."

Right then, Iron appeared from the hallway. "Don't forget the weapons. Clepsits don't have many of those, certainly none like the ones the voracans and I have been working on." He pushed his way to the center of the room, placing himself in front of Isaac. "Who cares if some misinformation has gotten us here? We are in a strong position. Anyone who stands against us will fall with the humans."

An awful stench polluted the air. Voracans poured into the room. They filled every available space, wedging themselves between the clepsits, their quills cutting anyone who didn't move out of the way fast enough.

"Join me now!" Iron bellowed.

An elbow prodded Wren's side. She turned her head. Isaac was mouthing something. *The device.*

The electro-no-ception device! She turned it on.

Undisturbed by the device, the voracans continued to prod the clepsits. Several extended their long proboscises—the sharp tubes used to take marrow from their victims. Apparently, the first fathers and mothers who refused to ally with them did not need to be saved for the chairs. They could be drained—killed—right now.

Wren changed the setting on the device . . . to no effect.

"Help!" someone yelled, but the voice hadn't come from any of the people under attack. It had come from the hall outside the room. "Help, everyone!"

Iron reached into the hallway and grabbed the noisy interloper.

Coney.

Wren ran up to Iron and kicked him in the shin. "Let Coney go!"

Iron turned to her, snarling, as if noticing her presence there for the first time. "What is that thing in your hand?"

"Nothing." She adjusted the controls again, still trying to find the right setting, still skeptical that the thing even worked.

Iron knocked it from her hands.

Wren tried to grab it from the floor, but Iron swatted her out of the way and into the nearest voracan. Its many spikes cut her skin. Its one flexible quill reached around her body, finding the perfect spot to puncture her flesh and drain her marrow.

She screamed.

Iron laughed. "Not as tough as you thought, are you?"

Coney dived for the device.

"Press the button!" Wren yelled, unsure if it would matter. Would Coney understand what to do? Clepsits didn't normally use buttons, not this kind.

He did. He pressed the button. Nothing happened. He pressed it again, again and again and again, but it did no good.

Wren felt the voracan slide its flexible quill under her skin, into her hip bone, sending a wave of fiery pain through her body.

Then the voracan released her.

Its body jerked. More quills jabbed her, but without purpose. She scrambled out of the way. "It's working, Coney! Don't press the button anymore."

"Give me that!" Iron commanded. He stepped forward to snatch the device from Coney's hands, but a flailing voracan got in the way. "Give that to me right now, boy, or I'll feed *you* to the voracans, too."

But the voracans posed little threat as long as Coney kept his grip on the device. He stood his ground.

"Do you want to get into trouble?" Iron roared. "*Real* trouble? Give me that thing right now, or you'll be banished from the clan."

Coney hesitated for the briefest of moments. Then, with a defiant tilt of his head, he said, "I don't care."

Kelp and Grace stepped in front of Coney, helping shield him.

Meanwhile, the voracans were writhing, their bodies twisting and turning in chaotic swirls, their quills snapping off as they collided with each other.

"Why aren't you attacking?" Iron demanded. When the voracans didn't respond, he approached the nearest one—the one that had attacked Wren. He tried to grab it, but his hand got caught and crushed, his bone snapping along with the creature's quills.

"Out!" Isaac said. "Get out!"

Aurora helped usher everyone into the hallway. Everyone except Iron.

They shut the door behind them, leaving the voracans and Iron inside.

Two days later the prison cells were empty, the humans and human sympathizers having been released.

Iron, who most agreed deserved a spot in a cell, was recovering in the hospital wing instead. Several humans kept watch over him. In fact, there were more guards than nurses.

The voracans that almost killed Iron couldn't be held in a cell with bars they could slip through so easily. Instead, a pit had been built specially for the creatures.

Isaac almost felt sorry for them.

"I can't stand the thought of having them nearby," Coney said. He, Isaac, and Wren were walking to the cafeteria for lunch.

"We need them around so we can test the new devices," Wren said. The new devices were like the prototype Justin had made, except they had only one setting—the one proven to interfere with the voracans' senses. These wouldn't have been possible to make without a voracan or two in custody.

Isaac definitely felt sorry for them. He'd been held captive while machines were built to destroy his species, so he understood the horror. No one deserved that.

"Do you think we'll let them go?" Isaac asked. "After they're done with the tests?" The device didn't have any permanent side effects, as far as anyone could tell, but that would only matter if the voracans were eventually freed.

"I don't know," Wren said, taking her place in the long line for food. "Some people have been talking about exterminating the voracans. Even now that Iron has been stopped, the voracans are still coming up to the surface to feed. Some people think exterminating them is the only way we'll be safe."

Isaac stood in line behind Wren and in front of

Coney. "You don't agree, do you?" She couldn't have. If she thought that, she would have destroyed the voracan babies when she'd had the chance.

"No. I don't know. That one voracan, Mine—do you still think it let us go on purpose?"

Isaac nodded. "I think so. Mine wasn't bad. He was nice, actually. We played games. We talked. I don't think the others are evil, either. They're just hungry . . . desperate. Maybe we could have gotten along if it wasn't for, for—"

"The chair?" Wren suggested. "Iron's plotting? Maybe we *can* get along one day, but in the meantime, I'm happy for my device."

Isaac had to admit that a part of him was thankful for it, too. It was the only thing that had stopped Iron and his army of voracans. A war would be waging without it, and in the end, that wouldn't be good for anyone—voracan, human, or clepsit. "I guess, but it should be a temporary fix—a safety precaution while everything gets back to normal."

The conversation lulled as they selected their lunch. Isaac chose pizza. Coney helped himself to some stew. Wren got a little of everything.

She licked her lips as they got to the dessert trays. "Human food is so amazing," she said, helping herself to a brownie, some apple pie, a chocolate chip cookie, and a cup of pudding. "I don't understand how everyone doesn't weigh a million pounds."

"Overeating is actually a big problem," Isaac said.

"Doesn't sound like much of a problem to me," Coney replied. He took a big piece of apple pie.

They sat down at one of the smaller tables. There weren't very many other kids around. Breeze and Bronco were sitting with some of the Antarctic clepsits. Mr. Read was sitting at a table with some other humans. Aurora was sitting alone.

"Where's Mrs. Read?" Wren asked. "Uh, my mom. Your mom." She still didn't know what to call her.

Isaac smiled. "Our mom. She had to leave the headquarters so she could talk to the humans in charge at Pacis. She'll be back in a couple of hours."

"What's she going to tell them?" Coney asked. His words were a bit muffled thanks to a mouthful of apple pie. He'd decided to start with dessert.

"Not the truth," Wren said. "Clepsits don't want to go to war with humans anymore, but that doesn't mean they trust them."

She was right. The clepsits and humans weren't even sitting together. They'd chosen separate tables so they wouldn't have to talk to each other.

"It isn't working," Isaac said.

"What isn't?" Wren asked. Her eyes widened. "The device? Are the voracans here?"

"No. The exchange." Isaac stood up and raised his voice. Everyone needed to hear this. "The exchange isn't working." The crowded cafeteria drowned out his voice. He climbed on top of his chair and shouted. "For generations, humans and clepsits have exchanged children to foster cross-species understanding, but it isn't working. The exchange can't work, not if no one wants it to."

Wren stood on top of her chair, too. "He's right. I've lived with clepsits my entire life. The exchange is supposed to help our species learn to accept each other, but all I've learned from most of my clan is hate and prejudice. How can we learn to accept each other when my own clan won't accept me?"

Bronco stood. "What are you saying? Do you want to end the exchange?"

"No," Isaac said. "I want to strengthen it. We need to let more humans know about the clepsits—humans like the boy who built the first electro-no-ception device."

"And we need to teach clepsits that humans are not dirty or violent," Wren added.

"We need to accept each other," Isaac continued. "To share the planet and work together, not just pretend we're doing it." Some of the humans in the room nodded, and several clepsits whispered words of agreement. Encouraged, Isaac added, "The voracans, too. They attacked because they were hungry, because they feared humans, and because Iron convinced them to. But we have to share the planet with them as well, and these devices will only keep them at bay until they come up with a way to counteract them. We need a better solution—a new food source for them, a treaty, maybe even another ambassador program."

Isaac stopped. The room had fallen silent, and no one was nodding anymore.

He didn't know what he'd expected—everyone to get up and start hugging each other? No, of course not. And perhaps he should have waited to bring up peace with the voracans. Everything he said was true, but it had been too much, too soon.

Amid the tense silence, he sat.

But then Coney started clapping. Then Bronco clapped. Slowly, applause filled the room. It hadn't been too much, too soon, after all.

Pigeons had taken advantage of the broken window. When the Reads returned home—after traveling by airplane, not rail—they found several of the birds living in the kitchen.

"Squatting squab," Mr. Read said, already shooing them outside.

"Come on." Isaac grabbed Wren's hand. "I'll show you around."

"I've already seen your house." She pointed to the broken window. "I'm the one who did that, remember? Uh, sorry, by the way."

"It's all right, dear," Mrs. Read said. "Why don't the two of you go out to the backyard?"

"Can we go to the park instead?" Wren asked. She was the one who'd insisted that they fly. "I told Sara, Justin, and Ryan we'd be there."

"Oh, yes, I suppose that's fine. Isaac, are you feeling up to that?"

"Yeah." He still had some scratches and bruises, but they weren't bad anymore. He'd had plenty of time to heal back at the headquarters while Mrs. Read tried to smooth things over with the human authorities. She'd finally convinced them that Iron's takeover had been nothing more than a publicity stunt for an upcoming film, but only after she'd put together a film company to produce it.

And he was excited to see Justin, Ryan, and Sara. The clepsits were fine with them knowing the truth— mostly because they'd built the electro-no-ception device, but also because most people agreed with what Isaac had said. They needed to revamp the ambassador program. They needed to build stronger relationships between species.

They needed real friendships, Isaac thought. Not temporary ones.

Isaac and Wren left for the park. A gentle breeze cooled the otherwise warm Tuesday afternoon.

"Have I told you about the Internet yet?" Isaac asked.

"Yes. You showed me all those cat pictures."

"Oh, yeah. So is Breeze the first mother of the Snow Clan now?"

Iron was awaiting trial, and Aurora had stepped down as first mother. Unless Isaac had completely misunderstood Wren's explanation of clepsit ranking, that meant the second mother got promoted.

"Yes," Wren said, grinning. "And Bronco is the first father."

"So everyone will have to be nice to you, right?"

Her grin got even bigger. "Uh-huh."

They'd reached the park. "I guess I should let them know we're here," Isaac said.

"I already texted them."

"You know how to text?" Isaac asked.

"I figured it out on my own. It's pretty easy. There they are now." Wren waved, and Sara, Ryan, and Justin ran over.

They told them everything that had happened. By the time they were done, the sun had almost finished setting, and the cool breeze had turned cold.

Ryan looked at the orange-and-pink horizon. "Are the voracans still a threat?"

"Not really. But we have this just in case." Wren removed an electro-no-ception device from her pocket and handed it to him. "It's based on Justin's design, but fixed on the right setting. They've been making lots of them at the headquarters."

"But we're not going to need them forever," Isaac added. "Some of the people at the headquarters are working on a new food source for the voracans." Mine was working with them, too, and had gotten the voracans to agree not to feed on humans or clepsits in return.

"Are you staying here?" Sara asked.

"No," Wren said. "I'm just visiting for a couple of weeks. Then I need to go back home." She looked happy about it.

"And I'm going to visit her at the burrow later this summer," Isaac said. "We're going to visit each other a lot from now on."

"Definitely. For a while I wasn't sure whether I belonged in the human world or the clepsit world, but now I know. I belong in both."

"It's all the same world," Ryan pointed out.

Wren nodded. She'd been using that gesture a lot over the last few days. "The next time I come to

Salmon City, Coney can come with me—only I guess you won't be in Salmon City anymore," she said to Isaac. "Because you have to move around so much?"

"Actually, I talked to my parents, and we're going to stay in Salmon City. Not year-round, of course." He still had his seasonal changes to deal with. No one minded that Sara, Ryan, and Justin knew, but Isaac couldn't start spilling the secret to everyone. Not yet, anyway. Full acceptance between the two species was going to take time. "We'll move in the winter, but next year we'll come back to Salmon City."

It had been his idea. He was going to have more say in a lot of decisions from now on, especially when it came to the ambassador program.

"You'd better," Sara said. "Your family moving here is by far the most interesting thing that's ever happened in Salmon City."

"Yeah," Justin said, and Ryan nodded. "You have to come back."

"I will." And why wouldn't he? He would finally have a reason to return. People were waiting for him.

"We want to visit the burrow, too," Sara added. "Justin and Ryan and me. Do you think people who weren't raised in the exchange program could become ambassadors? Or assistant ambassadors?"

"Maybe," Wren said. "Isaac and I are going to need as much help as we can get."

She was right, Isaac realized. They had avoided war this time, but tensions remained high. Maintaining peace wouldn't be easy. They would need all the help—all the friends—they could get.

Things were going to change. Isaac and Wren were going to change them.

©Trent Black

Laurel Gale lives with her husband and their own tiny monsters—also known as ferrets—in Vancouver, Washington. The idea for her second book started with the two main characters, Isaac and Wren. Laurel wanted to write about children from very different cultures—different species, in fact—growing up in each other's worlds, and the interesting challenges they would face. She loved the idea of tackling contemporary issues in a monster-filled fantasy. Laurel is also the author of *Dead Boy,* which *Reading Rainbow* called "a magical and mythical story of loneliness, courage, friendship, and living life to the fullest—even when you aren't technically 'alive.'" You can visit Laurel online at laurelgale.com.